SW

CREATURE OF THE NIGHT

Also by Kate Thompson:

The Switchers Trilogy
Switchers
Midnight's Choice
Wild Blood

The Switchers Trilogy (3 in 1)

The Missing Link Trilogy
The Missing Link
Only Human
Origins

The Beguilers
(CBI Bisto Award 2002)

The Alchemist's Apprentice
(CBI Bisto Award 2003)

Annan Water
(CBI Bisto Award 2005)

The New Policeman
*(Guardian Fiction Prize 2005, Whitbread
Children's Book Award 2005, Dublin Airport
Authority Children's Book Award 2005 and
CBI Bisto Award 2006)*

The Fourth Horseman

The Last of the High Kings

CREATURE
OF THE NIGHT

Kate Thompson

THE BODLEY HEAD
London

CREATURE OF THE NIGHT
A BODLEY HEAD BOOK
Hardback: 978 0 370 32929 1
Trade paperback: 978 0 370 32930 7

Published in Great Britain by The Bodley Head,
an imprint of Random House Children's Books
A Random House Group Company

This edition published 2008

1 3 5 7 9 10 8 6 4 2

The Random House Group Limited supports the Forest Stewardship
Council (FSC), the leading international forest certification organization.
All our titles that are printed on Greenpeace-approved FSC-certified paper
carry the FSC logo. Our paper procurement policy can be found at
www.rbooks.co.uk/environment.

Mixed Sources
Product group from well-managed
forests and other controlled sources
FSC   www.fsc.org Cert no. TT-COC-2139
© 1996 Forest Stewardship Council

Set in Sabon

RANDOM HOUSE CHILDREN'S BOOKS
61–63 Uxbridge Road, London W5 5SA

www.kidsatrandomhouse.co.uk
www.rbooks.co.uk

Addresses for companies within The Random House Group Limited
can be found at: www.randomhouse.co.uk/offices.htm

THE RANDOM HOUSE GROUP Limited Reg. No. 954009

A CIP catalogue record for this book is available from the British Library.

Printed and bound in Great Britain by CPI Mackays, Chatham, ME5 8TD

For Knute Skinner, my first publisher.

*Thanks to Mel, Jan, Lucy, Cillian and Dib
for reading the manuscript
and giving me useful advice.*

1

I told my ma I wouldn't stay there. I told her when she first came up with the idea and I told her again when she tried to bribe me with the new Xbox. I said it to her all the way down on the bus. Every time she opened her mouth to talk to me I said it:

'I'm not staying down there. You can't make me.'

So after a while she stopped trying to talk to me and she just talked to Dennis, showing him cows and sheep and tractors out the window of the bus. He liked the tractors but he didn't know what to make of the cows and sheep. He stared at them like they were something out of another world.

Which they were.

Our new landlord met us at the bus station in Ennis. His name was PJ Dooley. When he seen how much stuff we had with us he made a joke and said he should have brought the trailer.

I said, 'Ha ha,' and my ma gave me a savage look.

'It's mostly theirs,' I said to him. 'I'm not staying.'

PJ Dooley looked at me and then at my ma, and Dennis said, 'Can we go in the car?' and everyone started piling in the suitcases and plastic bags and backpacks. There wasn't much room left by the time me and Dennis tried to squash into the back.

'Take him on your knee,' my ma said, but I didn't want him on my knee and I shoved him over on top of a big bag of duvets and pillows. He laughed and wriggled himself comfortable and said: 'We going in the car!'

My ma didn't have a car. She said there was no need for one where we lived because we could go everywhere on the bus, so Dennis had hardly ever been in a car before. I was in cars all the time, though. Most weekends and some week nights as well, me and the lads would get hold of one. Sometimes we robbed two and raced them against each other out on the ring road or around the estates. That was class. It was what I lived for, the cars, and the Saturdays in the town centre, and what we bought with the money we got.

That was why my ma wanted to move out of Dublin. She told me it was only for the summer, to see how we liked it, but I didn't believe her. We'd given up the flat for one thing, and if we wanted to get one again we'd be right back at the bottom of the housing list. So I knew she had no intention of going back. She was moving for good to get me away from my bad-influence friends.

I thought that was her reason, anyway, and maybe it was part of it. But she had another reason for getting away from Dublin as well. I should have guessed it, I suppose, but I didn't. If I had I'd have told her it wouldn't work. Those people would be bound to find her in the end, wherever she went.

2

There was an old Skoda parked in the drive in front of the house.

'I'll be moving that,' PJ said. 'The last tenant left it behind him when he went. I don't suppose it's worth much.'

I nearly told him not to bother moving it because I would move it for him, all the way to Dublin. I could see it had no alarm in it, and I knew you could hot-wire those old ones. Beetle would know how to do it. I couldn't believe my luck. A ready-made escape sitting on my doorstep. If I could get money for petrol I was sorted already.

The house was a kind of cottage with an upstairs tacked on. It looked OK from outside, if you like that sort of thing. A big thick green hedge. Flowers in old buckets. But the front door was swollen into its frame from the damp and PJ had to put his hip against it to open it. Inside it was more like a shed than a house. It was no warmer than it was outside and the air was so damp you could nearly drink it. There was a little porch with mould growing on the walls and a bathroom opening off one side of it, right opposite the front door. Then two more doors opened off it, one into a sitting room and the other into the kitchen. There was a big old range in there, and stairs running straight up out of the room, and the back door at the bottom of them. Behind the chimney pipe the wall was covered in black streaks.

PJ said, 'It's soot. These old houses. Nothing you can do about it.'

Upstairs was much newer. There was a landing and three bedrooms, all with wooden walls, painted the colour of pus in a scab. The beds were old and knackered, and there were chests with sticking drawers and wobbly lockers and a dressing table with a swivel mirror that stared up at the ceiling.

In the biggest bedroom my ma said to me: 'You can have this one, Robert. We can set you up a desk in here.'

'A desk?' I said. 'What would I want with a desk?'

'For your schoolbooks,' PJ said, all innocent. 'For your homework and all. I'll find you a desk, leave it to me.'

'Homework?' I said. 'You said we were only staying for the summer.'

Behind his back my ma shook her fist at me.

'And anyway,' I said. 'I told you. I'm not staying.'

My ma made a vicious face. We followed PJ into the middle-sized bedroom and she said: 'I'll have this one. I like the view.'

The smallest one was just like a short corridor with a sloping roof as one wall. My ma said to Dennis: 'And this can be your bedroom. What do you think of that?'

'No!' Dennis wailed and clung to my ma's leg. 'Don't want a bedroom. I want to go home!'

He was still bawling when we followed PJ back downstairs, and my ma had to carry him and shout over his head.

'It's fine, honest. It's gorgeous. We love it.'

PJ opened the cupboard under the stairs. It was crammed full of boxes and bin bags.

He said, 'I hope you don't mind. There's some stuff here belonging to the last fella.'

Dennis said, 'Don't want a bedroom!'

PJ said, 'Only I didn't know what to do with it. I didn't like to throw it out. He might come back for it some day, you never know.'

My ma looked alarmed.

'Oh, there's no need to worry,' PJ said. 'He's an awful nice fella. A real gentleman. Lars, his name is. Swedish. But he left a bit sudden, like . . .'

'Why?' my ma said.

PJ shrugged. 'No one knows. He just disappeared one day.'

My ma looked even more alarmed, but PJ said: 'It's nothing to worry about. The police were here and they had a look around, but there was nothing suspicious. He took his passport and his driving licence and all, so he must have had a plan. It was just a bit sudden, that's all.'

'Did he owe you rent?' I said.

'He did,' PJ said, 'but not much. I wouldn't say that had anything to do with it.'

'Well we do, too,' my ma said. 'I should give you the deposit.'

She tried to put Dennis down but he turned up the volume. Normally he wouldn't dare. My ma would knock six kinds of shite out of him for that kind of carry-on, but he knew she wouldn't do it in front of a stranger. She had to pick him up again.

'No bother, no bother,' PJ said. 'Some other day will do fine. You settle yourselves in now and get unpacked.' He pointed out the window. There were two big meadows on the side of the hill, and above them a couple of houses and loads of sheds – a real farmyard from the looks of it.

'That's my house there, the two-storey one. If you need anything just call up. Anything at all.'

He gave me the keys. We'd all been following him since we got off the bus and we followed him now, when he went outside. At the door of his car he stopped and turned back to us.

'I'll send Colman down to you some day,' he said to me. 'He's about your age.' Then he looked at my ma and said, 'You might get a visit from my mother as well. She likes to know what's going on. She comes out with some strange things sometimes, but don't mind her. She's getting on.'

He got into the car and drove away. My ma waved after him, then took Dennis's hand and waved it as well.

He had shut up now that his protection was gone.

'Can you believe that?' she said to me. 'No deposit, no rent, nothing. We could do anything. We could rob the place. We could set fire to it.'

'Don't be putting ideas in my head,' I said. But I was as surprised as my ma, really. I don't think either of us had ever been trusted by anyone before.

3

It was June and the weather was warm but the house felt cold because of the damp and my ma set about lighting the fire. I put on the kettle and went out the back door. My ma heard me go out.

'Where you going?' she called after me.

'Back to Dublin,' I said.

'You are not!' she screeched at me. 'Come back here!'

'You can't watch me every minute of the day,' I said, and closed the door behind me.

I went round the front and had a look at the Skoda. One of the back tyres was low on air and there was green moss growing on the rubber round the door frames, but apart from that it looked OK. I wondered how long it had been sitting there waiting for the mystery man to come home. I wondered whether there was any charge left in the battery. The drive had a bit of a slope and the road did, too, if you turned left. I would probably be able to get up enough speed to jump-start it, once I'd got in and got the wiring sorted. I'd have to pick my moment, though; some time when my ma wouldn't miss me for a while. I hoped PJ wouldn't be in too much of a hurry to move the car.

Beside the house was a small grassy kind of yard with a hayshed and a block of little stone sheds. Behind them, on the other side of the fence, was the first of the two big meadows between our house and the two up at PJ's. They were the only houses in sight. In every other direction there was nothing but boring farmland.

I lit a fag behind the hayshed, out of sight of the house. My ma smoked herself so she never got the smell of it off me. I sometimes wondered why I bothered to hide it from her. It didn't bother me when she went ballistic. Not any more, anyway. I just ignored her. But I couldn't handle it when she got upset and cried. That happened a lot. It made me want to break things. Sometimes it made me want to break her.

The cattle in the far field lifted their heads to look at something, and I seen someone coming over. She was a long way off but I could see grey hair, a brown dress and wellies. I had a good idea who she was. I stepped into the shadow of a big green bush and took out my phone.

how do u hotwire a skoda

I sent the text to Beetle, then finished my fag and went back into the house.

My ma was in a rage. She had unpacked the bag of groceries we brought with us and all the eggs were broken. Now she had the sausages on the pan but she couldn't get the gas to light.

'I can't find a meter or anything,' she said. 'You look, will you?'

I looked at all the walls and then I leaned over the cooker and looked behind it.

'It's not going to be down there, is it?' she said.

It wasn't, but there was an orange pipe that disappeared into the wall. I went outside and found a gas bottle there and flicked the switch on top of it. The fat old woman was crossing the near meadow now, and I could see she had a dog with her.

'It's working!' my ma said. She was cheered up now. 'What did you do?'

'Turned it on,' I said. 'And we're getting a visitor.'

'Who?'

'Mrs Dandy, I suppose.'

'Mrs Dandy?'

'PJ's ma.'

'Dooley,' she said. 'It's not Dandy, it's Dooley.'

'Yankee Dooley Doodle Doody Dandy,' I said. 'Who gives a fuck?'

She laughed and I turned away so she wouldn't see the smile on my face. I wasn't ready to forgive her yet for dragging me down here.

4

Miraculously, Mrs Dooley had brought us a box of eggs.

'You must be psychic!' my ma said, showing her the broken ones in the bin.

'Good riddance to bad rubbish,' Mrs Dooley said. 'These ones are from our own hens, fresh laid. Save your scraps in a bucket and send the young lad up with them. Bits of old bread or potatoes or cabbage. They'll eat anything.'

Dennis stood in the doorway, watching the dog. It had gone under the table and laid down like it belonged there.

'Watch him,' I said. 'He'll have your hand off.'

'What, have your hand off,' Mrs Dooley said. 'Don't take any notice of him. That dog wouldn't hurt a fly.'

Dennis smiled, but he didn't come in.

'You might have to hunt him out of here the odd time,' Mrs Dooley said. 'He's always lived here and he doesn't get on with our own dogs above. Just send him home.'

She took a carton of milk out of her bag and gave it to my ma.

'And did your cows lay that as well?' I said.

Mrs Dooley looked at me a minute, then looked at

my ma. 'We don't keep milking cows no more,' she said. 'Too much trouble.'

Dennis decided it was time to chance his luck. He came in and stood in front of Mrs Dooley.

'I don't want a bedroom,' he said.

'Of course you do!' Mrs Dooley said. 'Why wouldn't you? Big boy like yourself.'

Dennis gaped at her.

'What age are you?' she said. 'You must be five or six at least!'

'He's only just four,' my ma said. 'But he takes age six in clothes.'

'He does, I'd say,' Mrs Dooley said, talking to my ma but still looking at Dennis. 'He's very tall.'

'They both are,' my ma said. 'Robert's only just fourteen.'

Mrs Dooley gave me a quick look over. 'Well,' she said. 'If you ask me they both need bedrooms and they're lucky to have them. Do you know how many children I reared? And my house no bigger than this one?'

Dennis just stared. He had no idea what she was talking about.

'Eleven,' she said. 'Eleven children in a house no bigger than this one. And there was no talk of any of them having their own bedroom!'

'Don't want a bedroom,' Dennis said again, but quieter this time.

My ma said, 'Did you really have eleven kids?'

'I did,' Mrs Dooley said. 'But there was only ever one child in this house, more's the pity, and she was never allowed out.'

'Why not?' I said.

Mrs Dooley looked at Dennis. He was staring at her with big, wide eyes.

'It's a very strange story,' she said, 'and a very sad one. But it can wait. Your dinner's nearly ready. I only came down to leave you the eggs and to make sure you put out a drop of milk for the fairies.'

'The what?' my ma said.

'Oh, I know you'll scoff,' Mrs Dooley said, hauling her fat frame out of the chair. 'But the truth is there was never a time since this house was built that there wasn't milk left out for the fairies. It's set on a fairy path, they say, between the fort over there' – she pointed out the window, across the road – 'and the other one over on our land.'

I couldn't look at her. I turned away and faced the cupboards, messing with the flex of the kettle. A grin was splitting my face. I wished the lads were here to see this.

'You might laugh,' she said to my back, 'but it's bad luck to disregard them.'

I heard her open one of the presses beside me and out the corner of my eye I seen her put a little green bowl on the table.

'About this much,' she said, pouring milk from the carton. 'Leave it on the windowsill when it gets dark.'

'All right,' my ma said. I could tell she was trying not to laugh as well.

'Lars used put it out every whole night,' Mrs Dooley said. 'And if he was away he would tell me and I'd come down and do it. That's why it's so strange. Him to disappear like that without telling a soul.'

My ma was stirring sausages beside me. I could see the smile on her face and I didn't dare look at her.

'I'll leave you to it, so,' Mrs Dooley said. 'Be sure and call over if there's anything you need.'

'I will,' my ma said.

'Come on, Bimbo,' Mrs Dooley said to the dog. But the dog was very comfortable under the table and it wasn't going anywhere.

It was more than I could take. I burst out of the back door, raced to the hayshed and laughed until my ribs hurt.

5

Mrs Dooley stayed for another few minutes, but I didn't go back into the house until I'd watched her, minus the dog, plod all the way across the first field. By then I'd done enough laughing and remembered that I was still mad at my ma. When I went back in the first thing I seen was the dog, still under the table.

'She says he'll go home when he's hungry,' my ma said, 'so long as we don't feed him. He used to belong to the old man who lived here and he still thinks it's his home.'

'What old man?'

'I don't know,' she said. 'But after he died they took the dog away with them, and then when Lars moved in he came back here.'

'The doggy likes it here,' Dennis said.

'Lars put in the dog flap,' my ma said. She was pointing at the hinged panel in the back door. I seen it there before but I didn't know what it was.

'I bet all that stuff with eggs and fairies was just an excuse,' I said. 'I bet she really came here to get rid of the dog. Scabby old thing.'

'Bimbo!' Dennis said. His mouth was full of hot sausage. 'His name is Bimbo.'

'Weird, isn't it?' my ma said. 'Can you believe it? In this day and age?'

She laughed. I gritted my teeth, determined not to join in. I picked up the little green dish and swallowed the milk.

'Hey!' Dennis said. 'You can't have that! You're not a fairy!'

'How do you know?' I said.

'Because I do.'

'I might be,' I said, and made a scary face at him. 'In the night . . .'

My ma put down my plate and poured me some tea. I was suddenly starving and I dragged up a chair. My ma put down her own plate and sat down.

'Bimbo!' Dennis said. He dropped his fried egg on the floor. The dog snapped and it was gone.

'Hey!' I said. 'You're not supposed to feed him!'

'I don't like the egg,' Dennis said. 'It's too strong.'

'But he'll never go home if we feed him. He won't get hungry.'

My ma surprised me. She said, 'I wouldn't mind keeping him. I never had a dog before.'

'Yes,' Dennis said. He dropped Bimbo a piece of bread. 'Yes, yes, yes, yes, yes!'

'What do you think?' my ma said.

I almost said yes as well, but I caught myself just in time.

'I don't care,' I said. 'I'm not staying.'

6

I told the lads that as well, when my ma landed me with the news.

'I'll just come back,' I said.

'Course you will, Robser,' Beetle said, and Fluke said, 'Where would we be without you?'

He was my cousin and I met the others through him when I was eleven, and they were all fifteen or sixteen. I couldn't believe it when they let me hang around with them. I couldn't believe I was in. But I was, well and truly. After that, me and Beetle and Fluke and Psycho Mick did almost everything together.

Weekends and school holidays we worked the streets, robbing bags and iPods and phones and stuff. I did most of the robbing because I was small and fast, and when we were making our way back out towards our own part of town, I carried all the stuff we'd robbed. There was a good reason for that. If the guards caught us, the others could all act innocent. I was Fluke's cousin and we just met up in town. How should they know what I was up to?

The guards never believed it, of course, but what could they do? They only caught us a couple of times, anyway. They dragged us off to the station and raked us over the coals and told us what kind of scum we were, but we just ignored it all. They called in our parents if they could find them and gave them a bollocking and told them to keep us off the streets. My ma tried, she really did, but what could she do? She couldn't make me a prisoner.

Nor could the guards, and that was the beauty of our system. I was too young for prison, and St Pat's and the other young offenders' institutions were all bursting at the seams with lads way worse than me. If we ever got caught in the cars it would be a different story, but we never did. Only the small stuff. We felt like no one could touch us.

One time when we were caught I got sent to some fella, a youth worker or something. I had to go and sit in his office and he asked me all these stupid questions about my home life and school and how I felt and all that shite. He said the other lads were exploiting me because of my age, but he didn't understand. I knew my place in the gang and I was happy with it. The others all had their places as well. Fluke was the oldest and kind of the leader. He called most of the shots, and he had the contacts for selling the stuff we robbed. Beetle knew where to score the good gear, and he had a talent for nicking car keys off pub tables or out of jacket pockets. And Mick was the psycho. He was seriously hard. One time when I was legging it with a woman's bag a fella on the street tried to stop me. He never knew what hit him. Mick moved in and slammed him up against the wall and knocked his teeth out, and then jumped on his head a couple of times when he was down. It scared me a bit, but the others said that fella was a stupid bastard and he should mind his own business. They said he had it coming, and we all got a great laugh reading about it in the papers.

So when Fluke said, 'Where would we be without you?' I knew he meant it. We were a fighting unit, an oiled machine, and every one of us was needed.

7

I kept checking my phone but there was no answer from Beetle. Maybe he was off his head, or maybe he was looking up Skodas on the Internet or something. After our dinner my ma took Dennis upstairs and began to unpack his stuff in his little bedroom. The floors in that house were as thin as the walls and I could hear every word they were saying. She asked him where he wanted to keep his Lego and his football jerseys and where Jim-jam the pyjama rabbit was going to sleep. Her questions were happy and bubbly but his answers were nervous and quiet. He still wasn't sold on the bedroom idea.

He never had his own one in Dublin. We had a poky little two-bed place. A while ago my ma wanted Dennis to move into my room with me but I wasn't having it. He was her brat, I told her. If she didn't want him she should have thought twice about getting herself pregnant.

She chucked me out when I said that. I was supposed to be grounded at the time so it was just what I wanted. I met up with the lads and we went and got a couple of cars. That was a good night, that was. One of the best. It made me smile to think about it.

I could only get one channel on the TV, and that was RTE2. All the others were just fizz and white scratches. I turned it off and looked at my stuff piled in the corner and decided I might as well unpack it, even though I wasn't staying. I wouldn't be taking much of it with me when I left, anyway.

I went upstairs, dragging two bin bags behind me. I heard Dennis say: 'I sleep in here tomorrow, Mammy. Just stay in your bed tonight.'

I paused on the stairs and waited for her reaction. I knew she really really wanted her bed to herself.

'All right,' she said. 'But only tonight. And if you wet the bed I'll murder you.'

Which, I thought, pretty much guaranteed that he would. I remembered that from when I was his age. Lying awake in terror, afraid to go to sleep in case I wet the bed. At that time I was still afraid of my ma's rages. They don't scare me now, but they scare Dennis. Poor little bollix. I almost felt sorry for the little rat.

'I won't,' he said. He was delighted with himself now. 'Jimjam bunny will wake me up in time.'

I remembered that trick of my ma's, too. My old Fuddy bear was lost years ago, but he still wakes me up sometimes when I need to piss.

Dennis was dancing around on the landing. When I got to the top of the stairs he said, 'Bobby! I sleeping with Mammy tonight. And then tomorrow—'

'Aren't you lucky?' I said. I pushed him out of my way. 'And listen, snotface. My room is out of bounds, OK? If I catch you in there you're dead meat.'

I went into it, leaving him staring after me. My ma came out of his room.

'Don't you talk to your brother like that!' she yelled at me.

'He's not my brother!' I yelled back, and slammed my door behind me.

Something swished and swung on the back of it. A pair of jeans and a denim jacket were hanging on a hook. I put down my stuff and went to look through the pockets. There was nothing in the jacket but in the left pocket of the jeans there was twenty euro and a handful of loose change, and in the other was a car key on a ring with a small little Swiss Army knife.

The key said SKODA.

I couldn't believe it. I punched air with my fist and stuffed the key and the money in my pocket, quick, in case my ma came in. I could see, now, what had happened. The chimney breast ran up through my room and the door, when it was open, rested flat against it. No one had closed it since Lars disappeared and the jeans and jacket had been missed. So if it was true that the guards had been called in, they hadn't done a very good job of searching the place. Why didn't that surprise me?

I didn't care. It was a gift. I didn't need to wait for Beetle's answer now. I would go that night, as soon as my ma and Dennis were asleep. I would still roll the car down the hill and as far away from the house as I could get before I started the engine, but there would be no messing around with clothes hangers or smashing steering locks. I would make a silent getaway, and by the time my ma noticed the car was gone I would be in Dublin.

Home.

I texted Beetle:

found key forget hotwire c u soon

Then I texted Fluke:

c u 2nite

I was bursting out of my skin with energy but I needed to be careful and not look too happy or anything. My ma would know something was up. So I took my time unpacking, yanking at the sticky drawers and hammering them back in. By the time I went back down I was in control of myself and giving nothing away.

My ma watched RTE2 all night, wrapped in a duvet with Dennis on her lap. The wind had got up and blew draughts in through the window frames and under the door. The fire blazed like there was a big vacuum cleaner up the chimney, sucking all the heat into the night. My ma kept putting more wood on it but the room was still cold.

I sat in an armchair, my eyes on the telly and my face set hard, but inside my head I was doing somersaults. I couldn't wait to get going in the Skoda. I hoped the radio worked. It would be tempting to put the foot down and boot it all the way up to Dublin, but I wasn't going to do that. I was going to chug along gently, sticking to the speed limits and stopping at red lights. I wasn't going to draw any attention to myself.

The air in the back tyre was a worry. I hoped it would get me there. No way I was going to stop at an air pump. If I had to get petrol it would be risky enough. I know I was tall for my age but I still didn't look seventeen.

'I wonder where we get the firewood?' my ma said when the ads came on.

'There's big logs in the hayshed,' I said. 'I'll cut some for you.'

'Will you?' She smiled at me. 'It's great having a man around the house.'

I stared at the ads, raging inside. I hated it when she talked to me like that. Trying to get round me.

'What will you cut it with?' she asked me.

I shrugged. 'Don't know. Can you lend me your nail file?'

She laughed. I leaned forward, put my hand in my pocket for some chewing gum, felt the car key in there. I smiled at my ma. She was over the moon. It was a long time since she'd had a smile from me.

She got it wrong, of course. She always did. She thought it meant I'd changed my mind and I liked it here. Liked being the 'man about the house'. She beamed back at me.

'Time you were in bed,' she said to Dennis.

'No!' he wailed.

'Do you want to sleep in my bed?' she said.

'Yes.'

'Then you go up now and wait for me.'

He didn't dare complain. She took him along to the bathroom and then up the stairs. Above the noise of the TV I could hear the wind thumping the roof. The whole house was creaking and grinding. Dennis would be terrified up there, but he wouldn't dare come down. My ma would kill him if he did.

When she came back she said: 'Why don't you get yourself a duvet? There's probably a late film on or something.'

She'd like that. The two of us snug and cosy on the sofa, watching a film. Herself and her little man. Like it was before Dennis came along.

'I don't want a duvet,' I said.

I didn't want to watch a film, neither. I wanted her to go to bed and go to sleep and leave the coast clear for me and the Skoda. A documentary came on and she rang her sister Carmel and talked for twenty minutes. When she was finished she rang her friend Maura and went over all the exact same stuff again. I don't know where she got the money for the credit. When she finally got off the phone she said to me: 'I think this is nice. This place. The countryside and all. And the dog.'

I didn't say anything. I watched more ads. My favourite cider. I could have murdered one.

'I don't know why you say Dennis isn't your brother,' she said.

My thoughts went haywire. Why did she always

have to do this? She had this stupid idea that if we weren't screaming at each other it was a good time to 'talk about things'. But 'talking about things' always ended up with us screaming at each other.

'Because he's not,' I said. We'd been here loads of times before.

'He is,' she said. 'He's your half-brother. It's the same thing.'

'It's not,' I said.

'It is,' she said. 'You're my son and so is he.'

'Yeah,' I said. 'But we don't have the same da, do we?'

'What difference does that make?'

'Because he knows who his da is, doesn't he? And I don't. Because you won't tell me. That's why.'

We'd been here before, too. A million times. She must have known we'd get here, once she started 'talking about things'. We always did.

She made a miserable face, like she was the one who was hurt by it and not me.

'When are you going to tell me?' I said.

'When you're older.' She always said that.

'I'm older now,' I said. 'I've been older for years! And I'm fed up with you telling me that. I don't see why it has to be such a big deal!'

Dennis called from upstairs. 'Mammy!'

Stupid kid. He'd get it in the neck, now. My ma was torn between tears and fury. I could see it in her face.

I couldn't stand any more. I did what I always did when she got like that. I stood up and went out.

8

But I wasn't prepared for what was out there with me. I stepped right into that wind that had been bashing around the house and it took my breath away and nearly knocked me off my feet. It was like my own rage, moved out from me into the world and destroying everything it came up against. It was like running into Mick when you weren't expecting it.

Everything that could move was moving. The trees, the bushes, the gutters, the phone and electric wires. You didn't get storms like that in Dublin. The wind was always broken up by the buildings and you only got hit by the little sharp bits that were left.

I ran for the hayshed, but it was groaning and shuddering like it was dying and I didn't trust it to stay standing. I ducked into one of the little sheds. The wind came in after me, banging off the walls and blowing into my face, but I managed to get a fag lit in the corner and just then that was the most important thing. I sucked at the smoke and felt the nicotine rush like an anaesthetic to my brain. Two more drags and the red fury dropped away. Two more and I could think again.

I was surprised that I didn't run straight for the Skoda and I was glad I didn't. My ma would have heard me go and called the cops, and I wouldn't have got twenty minutes down the road before they caught me. I needed to keep a clear head. You were useless for any kind of job if you lost the run of yourself. Me and my mates were good like that. We got off our heads after we'd had our kicks, never before.

I smoked the fag down to the filter and stubbed it out against the wall, then I stepped back out into the storm. Now that I was calmer I felt different about it. I began to smell things. Wet earth, battered leaves and grass, something else, like rotting wood, and every now and then a whiff of smoke from our chimney.

And then I realized it was something outside of me with a life of its own. This thing that was happening was nothing to do with me. It didn't even know I was alive. Out there in the darkness was a huge wild world that didn't care about cars and handbags and mobile phones. It was the first time in my life I'd seen it, but the weirdest thing was I had this feeling that I'd always known it was there, and that I'd been looking for it all my life. Working the streets, driving cars too fast, all those things were somehow about trying to find this wild darkness that was crashing through the world all around me.

For a few minutes I forgot all about myself and my troubles. I was afraid but excited, pulled right out of my own life by this bigger, stronger one. Then, suddenly, the excitement went out of it and I was just lost and alone, and I didn't even really know who or where I was. So when my ma's voice came through, roaring my name in the darkness, I didn't pretend I hadn't heard her. I fingered the key in my pocket and went back into the house.

9

I lay awake, listening to the storm and waiting till I was sure my ma and Dennis were asleep. I was still in my jeans and jumper, ready to step into my shoes and jacket and go.

I wished I had more money. I thought twenty euro would get the Skoda to Dublin, as long as it had enough petrol in it to get me to the nearest all-night garage. But what if twenty wasn't enough? I didn't really know what petrol cost. I'd never bought any. When we drove a car and it ran out we just burned it where it was.

I thought about all the money I'd robbed over the years. Most days we just got enough to get out of our heads, but once in a while we got lucky. I remembered a wallet bulging with fifties, and everyone's eyes out on stalks looking at them. And a woman's bag one time with a fat envelope inside with DEPOSIT written on it. That was when I bought my first Xbox and the flash trainers and the DVD player for the flat. My ma knew something was up and didn't let me out for weeks after it. It felt like weeks, anyway.

I could do with some of that now. If I had another fifty, even another twenty, I'd feel a lot happier. I thought about my ma's purse but I'd tried that once too often and now she always slept with it under her pillow.

Something was grinding against the wall above the window. A gutter or something, rubbing in its clamp. No fear of going to sleep with that racket. I was tired though, and I knew I had to stay sharp if I wanted my plan to work.

I listened to the house. There was no sound from my ma's room but I didn't think she was asleep yet. Not properly, anyway. Over the years I got an instinct about that. This wasn't the first time I'd sneaked out in the night. I'd had plenty of practice. Most times I was back in bed and asleep before daylight and she never knew I'd been gone.

Downstairs the dog barked, just once. It was a funny bark with a little yawny growl at the end, more like a welcome than a warning. Then I heard the bed springs creak next door and my ma, in a sleepy voice: 'Where you going?'

'Toilet,' Dennis said. 'Jimjam bunny woke me up.'

'Good boy,' my ma said. 'Good Jimjam bunny.'

I swore under my breath and turned over and pushed my face in the pillow. The landing light was always on because my ma was afraid of the dark, and I heard Dennis treading carefully down the squeaky stairs and then the click of the kitchen light switch. Then nothing. I was waiting for the sound of the bathroom door but instead Dennis said something, too quietly for me to hear, and then he was running back up the stairs.

'Mammy!' he said. 'I seen a little woman! Come and see!'

'What little woman?' She was mumbling, all drowsy, the way she always did when she'd taken a sleeping pill. I wished he'd shut up before he got her wide awake again.

'She was looking through the doggy door,' Dennis said. 'I seen her little face.'

'Did you?' my ma said. 'Was she a fairy?'

'She was little,' Dennis said. 'Little like me. But old. Older than you.'

Those words gave me a cold shock. I could see Dennis imagining fairies. But old ones?

'Come and see!' he was saying.

'Tomorrow,' my ma said. 'She's gone now. We'll look tomorrow.'

Dennis knew better than to argue, and I heard him climbing back into bed.

I sighed and began waiting all over again. The wind attacked the roof slates, sending clattery waves from one side of the house to the other. The grinding thing kept on grinding. Then my ma said: 'Dennis?'

'What?'

'Did you go to the toilet?'

Dennis said, 'Oh,' then it started again, the little footsteps outside my door, the squeaky stairs . . .

And then, I don't know how it happened, it was suddenly broad daylight.

10

I couldn't believe I'd let myself go to sleep. Once before I'd done it and I missed a good night out with the lads, but this was worse. What if PJ moved the car today? What if I'd blown my chance to get away in the Skoda?

I jumped up, as if I could grab the night before it got too far away and get back inside it. I sat on the edge of the bed, trying to rewind time and have another go at getting it right, but in the end I had to live with it. I'd screwed up.

Dennis was always up early. Usually he got himself some milk and biscuits and watched DVDs until my ma got up. She didn't get up before eleven and then she was always cranky. In Dublin I used to get out of the house before she got up. Some days I went to school. Some days I didn't. It depended on my mood and the weather, and what the others were doing.

But that day my ma was already up, and she was delighted with herself.

'We've had our breakfast,' she said. 'Will I put you on a rasher?'

I looked at the clock. It was half nine. On a Sunday.

'If you want,' I said.

She put on the kettle and opened the fridge. I stepped outside to see if my car was still there.

It was. The storm had passed over and the sky was cloudy but bright, like the sun wasn't far away. I looked around at the countryside, remembering how the wind had excited me last night, how it had made me forget myself for a while. But there was nothing interesting in it now. It wasn't even proper green, when you looked at it. It was kind of jaded, like every blade of grass had brown edges.

'We're going to mass,' my ma said when I went back in. 'I phoned PJ. It starts at eleven.'

'Mass?' I said. 'Since when did you go to mass?'

'I used always go,' she said. 'When you were small. And now we're starting a new life so we ought to go.'

'Well I'm not starting a new life,' I said. 'And I'm not going to mass.'

'Come on, Bobby,' she said. 'It's a good way to meet the neighbours.'

'We've met the neighbours,' I said, 'and they're all head-bangers.'

'They are not,' my ma said. 'And anyway, there are loads of other people in the village. You'll get to meet people your own age.'

'I won't,' I said. 'I'm not going.'

'Well you are,' she said. 'And that's that.'

'Just try and make me,' I said. I was already thinking about what I would do when she was gone. I was thinking it might be another chance to escape.

'Please, Bobby,' she said. 'Just for me?'

I put a tea bag in a cup and poured water on it from

the kettle. She wouldn't be gone long enough. Two hours max. It would take me four to get to Dublin. More if the traffic was heavy.

Dennis came and stood beside me.

'I seen a little woman,' he said. 'Just there.' He pointed to the dog flap. 'Peeping in, she was.'

'You're a head-banger too,' I said to him.

My ma fired the packet of rashers at me. It hit me in the neck.

'You can do your own fecking breakfast,' she said.

She went into the hot press that opened off the bathroom and dragged out an ironing board, and set it up in the middle of the kitchen, so I had to reach over it to put the rashers on the pan. She plugged in the iron and went upstairs, and came down again with one of my school shirts and a little grey suit.

I remembered the suit, and I remembered the time when I used to wear it. Like my ma said, she used to go to mass a lot, and I used to go with her. She would dress me in that suit and call me her smart little man. It was after we moved out from her ma's place and set up on our own. There was one time we used to go to mass nearly every day. Then I started school and after that I only went on Sundays.

When I grew out of that suit I got a blue one with pinstripes. How long ago was that, then? I remember we kept going for a while after Dennis was born, because I remember him crying in church when he was a tiny babby and my ma trying to shut him up. I don't remember his da ever coming with us, though. He used to stay at home in bed. And then he left, and after that my ma didn't go to mass any more.

I wonder if that was why she stopped going, because Paul left her. I never thought about it at the time. But I know that my ma changed after that, and she started using the sleeping pills and staying in bed half the day, and being cranky all the time, instead of just some of the time.

Maybe she was one of those people who needed a regular dose of religion. Maybe she really could start a new life down here, and start being happy again.

The grey suit smelled musty when she ironed it. I reached across her for one of Mrs Dooley's eggs. Why should I care, anyway, whether my ma was happy there or not? I wasn't going to be there to see it.

Half an hour later we had another fight. My ma said she wasn't going if I didn't go with her, and I said I couldn't care less and she marched upstairs and put the grey suit in the wardrobe and sat in the sitting room with her arms crossed. After about five minutes of that she got out of the armchair and called me all the names under the sun, and then she phoned Maura, and I went out for a fag.

When I came back in she had Dennis kitted out in the suit and she was scrubbing his hands and face with a dishrag. I remembered that, too, from when I was small. It hurt. But Dennis was too smart to complain, and too scared. My ma was in a foul temper. She always was when she couldn't make me do what she wanted.

When she went out the door she said to me, 'You'll go to hell.'

She said it like she wished it would happen. I watched her walk down the road, dragging Dennis by the arm. She hadn't gone more than a hundred metres before a car pulled up and offered her a lift. There was a couple in it, and two kids in the back. They weren't the Dooleys. I don't know who they were. Maybe everyone was like that around here. Like PJ with the rent. Trusting.

Too bad I wasn't staying.

11

As soon as the car had disappeared round the bend I started working on my new plan. I couldn't leave for Dublin while my ma was at mass, but I could still make good use of the time.

I unlocked the Skoda, got in, put the key in the ignition and said a little prayer. I don't know who or what I said it to, but it worked. The starter motor groaned then gave a big heave. There wasn't much life in it but there was just enough, and the engine started. I turned it straight off.

'You little beauty!' I said, patting the dash. Before I took out the key I checked the petrol gauge. It was nearly half full. More good luck.

I got out and looked around. There wasn't a soul to be seen except for myself. For a moment I almost panicked. I'd never been on my own like that before. I'd never been anywhere when there wasn't any people. But the nerves went away and suddenly it felt great. No one was around so no one could see me.

I unlocked the boot and found the spare wheel under the floor covering. There was a jack and a bag of tools parked inside the wheel hub but I had no idea how to use them. I'd never really used any kind of tools before. I knew how to break things, but not how to fix them.

I dragged everything out and closed the boot, then looked around again. Cows grazed and swished their tails. Bees buzzed. I wondered what everyone did here when they weren't going to mass. They must all be bored out of their brains. I could hear a car in the distance and I went round the side of the house and waited till it passed along the road and out of sight. Four more times during the wheel change I had to do that, but apart from that I wasn't disturbed at all.

I made things difficult for myself, I know that now. But I knew no better, not then. When I finally figured out how the jack worked I put it in the wrong place and the car fell off it twice. When I got it in the right place it worked like a dream and the wheel rose up off the ground like it was floating. I thought I had it made then, but with the wheel in the air and turning freely it was next to impossible to loosen the wheel nuts.

But I didn't rage and swear like I usually did when things went wrong. Instead I just got interested. People changed wheels all the time. I'd even heard of women doing it. So I looked at the wheel and thought about it and eventually I found a solution. It wasn't the right one, but it worked. I brought a breeze block from out by the sheds and chocked the wheel with it. Once it was stopped from turning I was able to get the nuts moving and they came off easily. One, two, three, four, five. I weighted them like treasure in my hand. I loved the feel of them, heavier than they looked. And the way they were shaped, tapering to nose their way through the hub and screw up snug and tight. I sat on the ground and looked at them for a while, and then I realized that anyone coming along the road could see the Skoda up on its jack, so I dragged over a couple of potted bushes to hide the wheel from the road.

I pulled off the flat and put the nuts inside the rim so I wouldn't lose them. I looked at the greasy plate underneath it with the bolts sticking out, and then I looked further in, at the rods and cables feeding in from the innards of the car. It was amazing.

I remembered the first time I drove a car. We'd nicked one in Drumcondra, a flash new Audi, and Beetle was driving. He was heading for the ring road to give it a proper burn, but Fluke told him to stop and let me have a go.

'Birthday present,' he said.

I was twelve years old and thrilled that my cousin had remembered.

Beetle moved over and I got behind the wheel. I was all for roaring off with squealing tyres like Mick always did, but I kept stalling it and the other three were falling around the place laughing. In the end I just chugged quietly through the back streets until a taxi driver passed us and looked at us a bit too long and hard, and then Fluke took over and we flew out of the place, burning rubber.

But after that I got loads of driving, and I got good at it. As good as any of the others. One time we got reported and the garda helicopter tracked us down. It was brilliant. It chased us along the main road, then I nipped down a side street and turned off the headlights and weaved through the rat runs until we shook it off, and then we ditched the car and ran.

Even Fluke was impressed by that. He said I'd passed my test at last. But in all those mad night-time drives I never once stopped to think about the nuts and bolts. A car was like an Xbox inside out. You pressed pedals and buttons and turned the wheel and that was it. It went.

I lay down under the Skoda but there wasn't much to see. More dirty wires and bars going into the front wheels. The mud-spattered floor. I got out and slid the spare wheel on to its bolts, put the nuts back, tightened them up, pushed on the hub cap. Everything fitted like it was supposed to. The jack let the car down gently.

It was ready to go. I stood back and admired it. I had four tyres with air in them, and I done it all myself.

12

The religion didn't cheer my ma up at all, not from what I could see, anyway. She was still mad at me and she wouldn't talk to me at all when she first came in. Except to say: 'Everybody else for miles around was there. I don't see why you think you're so special.'

She'd brought two big bags of shopping from the village and she banged around the kitchen putting things away, slamming the doors of the presses and swearing at the walls. Then she went into the sitting room and cried. I knew why she was crying. She wanted me to go in and say sorry. I used to do that when I was younger. I can't stand it when she cries, and I used to go in to make it better. Whatever it was I done I used to promise never to do it again, and then usually she would cheer up and say I was a great boy and all that crap. But I was wise to that now. At least if she was crying she was out of my face. I don't know why she still bothered. It was a long time since that trick had worked on me.

I made myself a cup of tea and sat in the kitchen, watching Dennis climb in and out through the dog flap. My ma had left her bag on the back of a chair and when Dennis was outside I robbed a fiver out of her purse. The next time he went out I took three fags from her packet and put them in my own. I didn't like her brand, but I was too poor to be choosy.

'Take the dog out with you,' I said to Dennis.

'Bimbo!' said Dennis. 'Come on, Bimbo!'

But the dog wouldn't go. I couldn't find any string so I cut one of the dishcloths into strips and knotted them together and tied it around its neck. My ma called me a vandal when she seen what I done but she was a bit pleased as well, to see Dennis playing with the dog. She was happier now, anyway. She always was when she'd had an old cry for herself. But she still hadn't forgotten about it.

'You should have come down,' she said. 'They're all really nice. The Dooleys gave me a lift home and waited for me while I did my shopping. They're gone home to have their dinner now but their young lad said he might call down later to see you.'

'Oh, good,' I said, but I think my ma missed the sarcasm.

'He's sixteen. His name's Colman. Quiet lad. Not like some.'

I went outside and looked at the Skoda again. It gave me a lift to see the wheel I changed. It looked a bit too clean compared to the others, but you'd have to look hard to notice it. I moved away quickly in case my ma seen me looking at it and got suspicious.

I didn't know what to do with myself. I was wired to the moon, ready to take off but stuck here for at least twelve more hours. I wanted another fag but I knew I'd want them more during the drive in the night and it would be better to save them. I resisted for about ten minutes, then gave in and had one anyway.

What did anybody do around here? What did my ma expect me to do when she dragged me down here? Run around in the fields picking daisies?

I went over to the sheds and poked around in them for a while. There were piles of junk in the smaller ones, mostly old farm stuff, completely knackered and useless. But there was a saw and an axe that looked like they were newer and they gave me an idea. There was a big stack of logs in the hayshed; just tree trunks, really, maybe four metres long. There was a pile of firewood at one end of them, but there wasn't much in it and the way my ma piled it on the fire it wouldn't last long. I didn't particularly want any more of her 'man about the house' shite, but I really fancied myself swinging that axe.

So after I'd had my dinner I got it out and took it into the hayshed. There was a chopping block at the front, a big thick slice out of a fat old tree, and I dragged one of the logs over and propped it across it. It didn't want to stay. Kept rolling off whenever I hit it. I wedged it with my breeze block but it still wasn't solid. The whole log jumped sideways every time I took a swing at it, and I spent more time picking it up and putting it back than I did cutting it. But in the end I got it secured and settled in to chopping.

It was harder than you'd think, though. For one thing you need to keep hitting it in the same place, which isn't as easy as it looks, and for another the axe didn't really bite into the wood the way I thought it would. It bruised it and flattened it, and now and then a chunk would fly out in a random direction, but I hadn't even got through one section of the log before I had to stop for a breather.

I turned round and seen my ma watching me. She smiled and opened her mouth but I knew what was going to come out of it and I said: 'Just shut it, all right? Before you start. Just leave me alone to get on with it!'

I didn't wait for an answer, just turned and picked up the axe again and started to swing like a madman at the wood. Bits flew all over the place, smacking me on the shins and the arms. I hacked and hacked until my heart was pounding like a road hammer, and when I stopped to rest again my ma had gone.

But there was someone else there. Colman Dooley. Leaning against the telegraph pole beside our gate. It wasn't a good start. He was watching me, and he was laughing.

13

'I'm Colman from up the road,' he said, coming into the yard. 'Coley, if you like.'

He was taller than me and a lot broader as well. Beefy. I let him take the axe from my hand. He looked at the blade.

'It's blunt,' he said, with a big grin and a laugh behind it. 'Completely useless. You might as well be hitting it with a lump hammer.'

I felt the blood in my face. 'I know,' I said.

'Come up to the house,' he said. 'My grandfather will sharpen it. He has the knack.'

I shrugged. 'I don't care.' I'd had my go with the axe and that was all I wanted. I didn't care whether the wood got chopped or not.

'Come up,' he said. 'He'll do it in ten minutes.'

'Don't bother,' I said, but he turned back towards the road with the axe in his hand and I found myself following him.

'Do you want to tell your mother where you're going?' he said.

'No,' I said.

His bike was leaning against the hedge. It was a fancy mountain bike with suspension. He picked it up and handed me the axe. We walked up the road, him pushing his bike and me with the axe on my shoulder.

'How far is it by the road?' I said.

''Tisn't far,' he said. 'About a mile maybe.'

'Your grandma came across the fields yesterday.'

''Tis shorter all right,' Coley said. 'But it's boggy. I didn't want to turn up in my wellies. You might have laughed at me.'

But he was the one who was laughing. Every second time he opened his mouth a laugh came out of it. I didn't like it. It felt like he was laughing at me. I wanted to knock the stupid grin off his face, but I kept my spare hand in my pocket where it was safe.

After another while he said: 'Sure, you weren't to know.'

'Know what?' I said.

'About the axe. Being blunt and all. How would you know about things like that? I don't suppose you see too many axes in Dublin.'

I shrugged. I wished he'd shut up about it.

'I might ask my father for the chainsaw,' he said.

I thought a chainsaw was a murder weapon. 'What for?' I said.

'Go through those old sticks like butter,' he said. 'We'd make short work of them.'

Coley told his grandfather my name was Robert. My ma must have told him that. She always did when she was trying to make an impression on someone, the stupid bitch. No one called me Robert, not even her. I got called

47

Rob, Robbie, Bob, Bobby, Bobser, Robser – so many names I sometimes forgot who I was. The one I liked best, though, was what Beetle called me sometimes. Roberto. It wasn't the name so much as the way he said it. He only used it when I did something really cool, like snatching the latest model Nokia or throwing off a garda car with a handbrake turn. Then he would say 'Roberto!' rolling all the Rs, like a ringmaster looking for applause for some brilliant acrobat or something.

'RRRoberrrrto!'

Maybe he'd say it tonight when I turned up with the Skoda. I felt the phone in my pocket. No texts from any of them. No calls to see if I was OK. But then, that wasn't our style. We only contacted each other when we were looking for action.

'You can call me Rob,' I said to Coley's grandda, but I meant it for Coley, really.

His grandda looked at the axe. Coley was grinning, but trying not to.

''Tisn't work, I suppose,' his grandda said, getting up out of his chair.

'Of course it's work,' his grandma said, coming out of the kitchen. 'But nobody seems to care any more. They even open the shops in Ennis on a Sunday now, can you believe that?' She was looking at me but I didn't know what she was on about and I just shrugged.

'Sunday is just like any other day now,' she said.

''Tisn't really work,' Grandda Dooley said again. He winked at me and went out the door. Me and Coley followed him out into the yard. There was any amount of buildings and barns out there, but he went to a row of small stone sheds, a bit like our ones only these were in better order. He unlocked a padlock on one of them and we followed him in. On one side were farm tools leaning up against the wall – forks, shovels, rakes, another axe and a pickaxe, sledgehammers, crowbars. On the other side was a smart workbench with rows of hand tools and a grinder, bolted on.

'Fetch a bucket of water, Colman,' he said. And then, to me, 'We used do it all by hand, you know, with whetstones. Very slow.' He looked at the axe again and laughed, just the way Coley did. 'This one would have taken me half a day. We'll do it in half a minute, now.'

He turned on the grinder and the wheel began to spin. Coley came in with the water and his grandda stood it on the bench beside the grinder.

'You'd better stand back now,' he said. 'And I'll have to find my goggles.' He laughed that little laugh again. 'There'll be a lot of sparks flying around. I'm blind enough already.'

He put on his goggles, dipped the head of the axe in the water and touched the side of the blade against the wheel. He was right about the sparks. A huge shower of them flew up from the steel, like a firework.

He dipped the axe in the water again and returned it to the wheel. Then again, and again, he dipped it and ground it and dipped it and ground it, and he only stopped when he took it over to the door to look at it in the daylight. It took a lot more than half a minute. It was at least ten minutes before he was happy with what he done, and then he turned the axe over and began again on the other side.

'''Tisn't as easy as it looks,' Coley said. 'I tried it once with a penknife. It turned pure blue. You wouldn't cut mud with it now.'

'We're getting there,' his grandda said. He took it over to the door again. 'We just have to get the burr off it now. See it there?'

I looked closely and seen what he was pointing at – a little rough ridge of metal running along the edge of the blade.

'We'll take that off with a small stone.' He clamped the axe in a vice and dipped a square pink stone in the bucket. It was smoother than the big round one on the bench grinder. He ran it along one side of the blade and then the other and he showed me the bits of the burr coming off on it, like grey sludge.

'That'll do it,' he said. He let the axe out of the vice and handed it to me. 'Keep it turned away from you now. We don't want any accidents.'

'You could shave yourself with that,' Coley said.

'You could,' his grandda said, 'if you had a very, very steady hand.'

They both laughed and this time I joined in.

14

I was itching to try out the axe but Coley followed his grandda back into the house and his grandma had tea ready, all laid out on the table with cups and saucers and cake and biscuits and milk in a jug, like something out of an old film.

Coley sat down but I didn't. I was thinking about a quick getaway.

'Sit down, sit down,' Grandma Dooley said. 'You'll have a cup of tea.'

And before I knew it I was at the table. There was something about Coley and his grandda, like they were going along with the flow instead of always against it all the time, and somehow I had to go along as well. I wasn't so sure about his grandma, though. She had sharper edges.

She said, 'Did you leave out the milk last night?'

I looked at Coley. He was grinning up at the ceiling. Sometimes I wondered if he was all there.

'I don't know,' I said. 'My ma might have.' I knew she hadn't.

'I hope she did,' Mrs Dooley said. 'I hope she did.'

'What would happen if she didn't?' I said.

She shook her head, all serious. 'Bad luck to upset the fairies. You wouldn't know what might happen.'

'Like what?' I said.

But she didn't answer that. She poured out the tea and Coley reached for cake. I did, too.

'Is the house all right for you?' she said.

I said, 'It's fine. Very nice.'

'Fierce wind last night,' she said.

'Fierce,' Mr Dooley said. 'Very unusual for the time of year.'

'You didn't lose any slates?'

'I don't think so,' I said.

'Good.'

We ate and drank. Mr Dooley sounded like a straw at the bottom of a milkshake. I could see Coley trying to hide his grin again but I kept a straight face. I had to. If I started laughing I'd never stop.

Mrs Dooley said, 'There was only ever one child reared in that house.' I wondered if she ever talked about anything else or if she was for ever stuck in the same groove, like the rabbit at the dog track. 'Fifteen years she lived in that house and nobody ever saw her. Nor her mother, neither. Himself used do all the shopping and suchlike. Things a man shouldn't have to be buying.'

I was reaching breaking point. I didn't dare look at Coley. I just kept my head down and stuffed my face with cake. But the next thing she said cured me very fast.

'They murdered her for a finish.'

'Murdered who?' I said. 'The child?'

Mrs Dooley nodded. 'So they said. Put them in prison and all. The two of them.'

'I don't believe they did it,' Mr Dooley said. 'They never found a body or any evidence or anything.'

'I don't know whether they did or they didn't,' Mrs Dooley said. 'But poor Peggy wasn't right in the head, that much I do know. Right from when the baby was born.'

'That can happen,' Mr Dooley said.

'It can,' Mrs Dooley said. 'These days they know how to treat it. I suppose they weren't used to it, then.'

Mr Dooley slurped his tea. 'She maintained it wasn't her baby at all,' he said. 'That was the start of it.'

'It was,' Mrs Dooley said. 'She swore it was a changeling.'

'What's a changeling?' I said.

'A fairy child,' Mrs Dooley said. 'Her baby stolen away by the fairies and their own child left in its place.'

'And was it?' I said.

But neither of the old people answered that. They looked at each other and they didn't say anything for a while, and then Mrs Dooley said: 'Poor Peggy never got out of prison. She died there. Joe came back and he lived out his days in the house. He was ninety-three when he died and I don't believe he enjoyed a single day of his life there without Peggy.'

'It's a great house, then,' I said. 'Full of happy memories.'

Mr Dooley and Coley laughed.

I said, 'How do they know the little girl lived for fifteen years if no one ever seen her? How do they know they didn't kill her when she was a babby?'

I wish I never asked that question. The answer creeped me out.

Mrs Dooley said, 'There was a nurse used call at the house every month. Mary Crowley was her name. She used see the child all right. But she would never talk to anyone about her. Whatever she knew, she took it with her to the grave.'

'And besides,' Mr Dooley said, 'we used hear her.'

Mrs Dooley nodded. 'She had this terrible little voice. You'd hear it sometimes, if you were walking past the house. There were words in it but the sound was too high pitched. Like a cat trying to speak. Calling for her mammy or whatever it was she wanted. But sharp, like, as if she was ordering, not asking.'

'You'd even hear it from here the odd time,' Mr Dooley said. 'The night-times were the worst.'

Grandma Dooley nodded again. 'Sometimes you'd think it was the sound of the wind, and then you'd realize there was no wind. Just this high shrieking, like something out of hell. You couldn't tell if it was pain or anger or both. There were times we used sleep with the pillow over our heads for fear we'd hear her.'

Mr Dooley said, 'Once you got that sound in your head there was no way you would sleep again that night.'

I thought they were winding me up and I looked at Coley, but he wasn't grinning any more. He said, 'I never knew that. You never told me about the voice.'

'We didn't tell you when you were smaller,' Mrs

Dooley said. 'We didn't want to scare you. And you wouldn't want to be telling your little brother, either,' she said to me.

'Nor my ma,' I said. 'She's bad enough as it is. She's terrified of the dark.'

Mrs Dooley looked at me like I had two heads. 'I never heard of a grown woman afraid of the dark before,' she said.

'I'm not afraid of it,' I said. But I was glad, all the same, that I wouldn't be sleeping in that house another night.

Coley's da was in the yard when we went back out. Coley asked him for the chainsaw and he gave me a long, hard look. Then he said to Coley, 'You know the rules.'

'I do,' Coley said.

'And you both have to stick to them.'

'We will,' Coley said. And then he said to me, 'You have to set the wood up right every time. And you have to keep the work area clear. And if you're not working the saw you have to stay four paces away. And you have to wear goggles all the time.'

They both looked at me, expecting something.

'Sure,' I said. 'Fine by me.'

We crossed another yard with more sheds and barns. In the open bay of a huge steel lean-to, the bottom half of a man was hanging out of the bonnet of a Land Rover.

'My brother Matty,' Coley said. 'He's a mechanic down in Ennis. At the weekend he fixes up old cars for a hobby. He's a greasoholic.'

'Cool Land Rover,' I said. I had a thing about Land Rovers and was always trying to rob one, but we never got the keys to one.

'It's mine,' Coley said. 'My uncle gave it to me. It needs a lot of work.'

'And can your brother fix it?' I said.

'He can fix anything,' Coley said. 'But I'd say I'll be married by the time that thing is up and running.'

'Can I see it?' I said.

'You can,' he said. 'But maybe some other day. If we don't get that wood cut soon the woodlice will have it all ate.'

As we walked back down the road, me with the axe and a can of petrol, Coley with the chainsaw, I said to him, 'Is it true? That story about the child?'

'It is,' he said. 'It's as true as that mountain is standing over there.'

But when I looked at the mountain I couldn't make it seem real at all. That whole place, with its smells and its sounds and its stories, was just like a long, green dream.

15

I was grand so long as it was light, but once it got dark the things Grandma Dooley said came back into my head. I got up and drew the curtains against the darkness, which was a thing I never done in my life before that.

My ma didn't notice. She was sat beside the fire, same as last night, under her duvet. There was one of those serial-killer films on the TV. There seemed to be one on nearly every night. If there was as many serial killers as there was serial-killer films we would all be dead inside a year.

'You'll give yourself nightmares,' I said to my ma.

'I know,' she said. 'But it's a good one, isn't it? I think the cop is doing it.'

I could see Dennis struggling to keep awake on her lap because he knew that once he went to sleep she'd carry him up and put him in his own bed under the sloping roof.

There was no wind that night but the house still made noises. Not big ones but little tiny ones. A click on the stairs. A scuffle in the roof. A rattle from the bathroom. The dog came in and sat by the fire, looking at my ma. I wondered if she'd remembered to feed it.

It was the thought of the child that gave me the

creeps, howling with pain and giving orders in the night. I kept thinking I heard her and I kept looking round at the door. What could have been wrong with her that they had to hide her away like that? And how did they kill her? What did they do with the body? What if it was still in the house somewhere?

Dennis was dozing, then jerking awake, then dozing again. The dog pricked its ears and sat up and looked towards the window. What had it heard? With a horrible shock I remembered I'd left the axe leaning up against the side of the hayshed. I meant to put it away but I'd ended up walking most of the way home with Coley and I didn't think of it again after I got back.

It definitely couldn't stay there. You never knew what kind of weirdos might be wandering around in the dark. I put my jacket on and went out. I thought I'd have a smoke but once I got out there I didn't want to hang around. The moon was out and looking at me. Something moved under the hedge.

I grabbed the axe. I was going to put it back in the small shed where I got it from, but what was the point of that? The psycho could find it there as easily as in the hayshed. And once he had it our back door would be matchsticks and we would be butcher's meat.

I looked around but I couldn't think of anywhere to put it where the psycho wouldn't find it. He was probably watching me right now. I didn't run, but the devil was behind me when I went through the back door and closed it behind me, and locked it.

I looked at the axe. What the hell was I going to do with it now? I couldn't leave it lying around in the kitchen because if he got in through the back door he would find it sitting there, like an invitation. So I took it upstairs with me and propped it up in the corner of my room.

During the next ad break my ma wrapped Dennis in the duvet and carried him upstairs. I thought he would wake but he didn't. She brought another duvet down with her when she came.

'My own bed at last!' she said. She settled back in and lit a smoke.

We were doing well. We hadn't had a row all evening, but now Dennis was gone there was a good chance she'd start talking again. So before the next ad break came on I took myself upstairs and lay in bed with the light on, listening to the screams and thuds and creepy music from the TV. But it wasn't long before it came to an end and I heard my ma flushing the toilet and coming upstairs.

She stuck her head round the door.

'I was right,' she said. 'It was the cop doing it.'

I said, 'Oh,' and she went out. But a couple of minutes later she was back.

'What did you do with that axe?' she said.

I nodded towards it and she seen it in the corner. She laughed and said, 'You're worse than I am!'

I couldn't help it. I burst out laughing, and for a delirious minute the two of us were giggling together like best friends, like we used to one time, in the dream time before Paul and Dennis came along. One bit of me didn't want it to be happening, but it felt so brilliant. I was doubled up on the bed and she was clinging to the door frame, trying to stay on her feet. But she had to spoil it. She always, always, always had to ruin everything. She couldn't leave it alone, just laugh and go. She came over and sat on the bed and said, 'Ah, my Bobby,' and she started trying to tickle me. Can you believe it? Tried to tickle me as if I was a little kid like Dennis.

I stopped laughing and tried to push her away, but she didn't get it. She thought I was playing, too.

'Get off me!' I said.

She lunged for my armpit, going, 'Bobby, Bobby, Bobby.'

I pushed her away again, vicious hard. I hurt her. She got up, all surprised and offended.

'I was only messing!' she said.

'Well don't,' I said. 'Don't fucking mess with me, all right?'

I seen tears start in her eyes and I turned myself over and pulled the duvet over my head. I listened to her footsteps. She didn't go into her room. She went across to Dennis's room instead, and when she came back the springs on her bed creaked and I heard her whispering and I knew she had brought Dennis in with her. For her sake this time, not his.

Then my own tears came. Not because I'd hurt her and not because she'd gone to get Dennis, but because

I'd let my guard down. I'd laughed with her and let her in. But you can't open yourself to one thing and not another. Once your guard is down everything is all in there waiting to come at you. The empty space where my future should have been. The pain. The whole big dirty mess of my life.

16

I didn't make the same mistake twice. An hour later I was outside the house, standing beside the Skoda, the key in my hand. It was creepy out there in the dark. I couldn't see my hand in front of my face and I kept hearing things – rustles and scratches and little thuds, like someone walking down the road or up the drive. I kept thinking the child was behind me. But I was used to being scared and I didn't mess up. It's impossible to open a car door in total silence, but I came close to it. I'd had plenty of practice.

I put the key in the ignition and turned it to free the steering lock, then leaned across the driver's seat and let off the handbrake. The car didn't move, and for a moment I thought the whole plan was a non-runner, but I leaned on the door frame and rocked her a few times and whatever was seized freed up and she began to roll. I jumped in, holding the open door with one hand and the steering wheel with the other, but she was rolling too slowly so at the bottom of the drive I got out again and gave her a hand, pushing against the door frame and steering with my left hand. She speeded up and soon I was running, and then I jumped in and let her freewheel until she was almost at the bottom of the hill.

I decided to try a jump-start – it would be quieter

than the starter motor. I put her into third and let out the clutch. She purred into life so quietly it was like she knew exactly what I wanted and was bending over backwards to help me.

At the end of the road I stopped to find the headlights switch, then I turned towards the village, and Ennis, and Dublin. I would never, as long as I lived, slag off a Skoda again.

I was scared shitless for the first while, watching for the guards, checking my speed, dipping my headlights religiously. But there were hardly any cars on the road and once I was past Ennis I began to relax and enjoy myself. I turned on the radio and thought about Coley and the chainsaw.

That was some brilliant machine. I couldn't wait to get my hands on it, but Coley did the first bit, to show me, and I split the chunks he sawed with the axe so they'd fit on the fire. Then he handed it over to me and I ripped into those logs like I hated them, and he was right – the saw went through them like they were butter.

After a while he made me take a break. He said it was to fill up the petrol, but I think he wanted to make me stop for a while as well. I hadn't noticed it, but when I went to let go of the chainsaw my fingers were stuck around the handles, like some kind of cramp. I had to stretch them a few times before they would work at all. My shoulders were cramped as well, and there was a pain in my neck and my back. Coley laughed at me.

'It's heavier than it looks,' he said.

I could still feel the pains now, sitting in the car. It proved I'd done something, and it wasn't just messing or killing time, neither. We'd cut enough firewood to last my ma for weeks.

On the far side of Limerick I stopped to get petrol. It was one of those twenty-four-hour places where you have to pay first before you put in your petrol. I almost drove straight on when I seen that, but then I was worried that I might run out before I found another one, so I got out and dropped my twenty euro through the little window and I tried to look casual and grown-up but the guy didn't really look at me at all. He looked tired and bored.

So five minutes later I was back on the road, loads of petrol in the tank, and nothing but the empty road between me and the lads.

17

I went straight to Fluke's and parked the car in a dark side street behind his block of flats. I'd passed a few garda cars but none of them had taken any notice of me and there were none around now. I was high as a kite. I'd made it.

I rang Fluke's number. He never set up his message box and the phone rang and rang for ages but eventually he came on.

'What's up, Bobser?' He sounded half asleep, and not too pleased.

'I'm outside,' I said. 'I've got a car.'

'Outside where?' he said.

'Outside your place. I need to get rid of this motor. Are you coming?'

'I'm not at home,' he said. 'I'm at my girlfriend's place.'

'Where's that?' I said. 'I'll come and get you.'

'Ah, fuck off, Bobser,' he said, and he hung up.

I swore at the phone. It wasn't the hero's welcome I'd expected. I knew Fluke had a girlfriend but she'd never got in the way of us before. Maybe that was because he usually called the shots and I just went along. I couldn't make it out. I'd only been gone two days. Things couldn't have changed that much in two days. I wanted to ring him back and tell him what I thought of him and his girlfriend, but I didn't have much credit and I didn't want to waste it. I sent him a text instead.

dickhead

Then I rang Beetle. Three times. And three times I got his answer message.

'Beetle,' was all it said.

I swore at the phone again. He was probably out cold. It happened all the time. He couldn't hold his drink, the wanker. If he had a skinful he just passed out and nothing you could do would wake him. The first time it happened we carried him home but it took us all night. After that we just left him on the street or wherever he landed up.

So that left Mick. He would be up for it. He was always wired and he hardly ever slept. His flat was just round the corner.

But after I phoned him I wished I hadn't. There was a manic edge to his voice that he sometimes got when he was out of his head on crack.

'Stay there, stay there, stay there, stay there,' he said. 'I'll be with you in two minutes. Two minutes.'

It was ten, though, and it left me too much time to think.

Why was I so keen to get rid of the car? Getting rid of it meant burning it out or driving it into deep water somewhere to hide it from the guards. But where was the point in doing that? I was missing and so was the car. There was nowhere I was likely to go except Dublin. The cops didn't need to put two and two together. They already had four. It would be far smarter for me to get out while I was winning and just walk away, instead of getting Mick involved. That was just asking for trouble.

He drove like a lunatic, even when he wasn't hammered. Speeding up the arse of other cars and pulling out at the last moment to overtake them. If something was coming the other way it was their look-out. We all ran red lights but the rest of us usually checked to make sure nothing was coming the other way. Mick didn't. If he seen a red light he put his foot to the floor. The nearer the miss the better he liked it. It was a miracle he hadn't already killed us all.

So I thought of just leaving the Skoda where it was with the keys in it, and making a quiet getaway. I could phone Mick in the morning and say the cops came along and I had to leg it. But he wouldn't believe me. And anyway, where would I go? I'd come up to be with the lads. Without them there was nothing for me here.

I tried staying in the driver's seat but there was no arguing with Mick when he was in that kind of mood.

'Move fucking over,' he said. He leaned in the door. He stank of burning chemicals. 'We'll take it out to Bray,' he said. 'We'll push it into the sea. Where did you rob it?'

I told him. He didn't remember I was gone to Clare,

even though I'd been talking about it for weeks. He put his foot down and scorched away up the street. Every time he changed down the gearbox made a sound like breaking bones.

'Fucking Skoda,' he said. 'Fucking heap of shit. Where did you rob this from?'

He asked me that seven more times before we got across the river. After the second time I stopped answering. I shut my eyes and hung on to the handle above the door. As if it could possibly save me. I wanted to put my seat belt on but me and the lads didn't do that. I'd never hear the end of it if I put it on now.

I don't know how we made it as far as Dalkey. We had a clear road, I suppose. Not much traffic around at five o'clock on a Monday morning. And the cops must have all been asleep. I never crossed Dublin before without seeing a garda car, at any time of the night or day.

I almost wished for one. The Skoda was shrieking with pain. Gears, engine, the brakes on the odd time when he thought of using them. I tried to get into the mood and make myself enjoy the ride but I couldn't. This wasn't like the other times when we were all together. Fluke or Beetle would always have got the wheel off Mick without pissing him off. They knew how to handle him, but I didn't. There was only one way this ride could end.

I seen it coming. There was a roundabout in front of us but Mick wasn't slowing down.

'Brake!' I yelled at him, but his foot was rammed to

the floor and he wasn't moving it. There was another car on the roundabout. It was nearly light but it still had its headlights on. The driver saw us coming and he jammed on the brakes and swerved, so the cars were side on when we hit and we both ended up on the grass in the middle of the roundabout, a few metres apart.

Mick had blood on his face but he was busting himself laughing. The other fella wasn't. He had a face like a tomato and he was already out of his car. I jumped out and tried to stop him. It was for his own sake but he wouldn't listen to me. He was roaring and shouting and he kept coming.

The door of the Skoda on Mick's side was bashed in from the crash, but he moved across to my side, fast and strong as an ape, and got out. He wasn't laughing now.

'I'll fucking burst him,' he said.

I shouted at the other driver. 'Fuck off! Get out of here! He'll kill you!'

But it was already too late. Mick put his head down and went at him like a bull.

I didn't stay to watch.

I ran.

18

I thought it was sweat running down my face but when I put up my hand to wipe it off it came away all blood. I went up an alley and stopped beside a garage door. There was a big lump just above my forehead and a gaping cut on top of it. I must have hit my head in the accident. I didn't remember. But I knew it wasn't too bad. I'd had plenty worse.

What worried me more was my left shoulder. I must have given that a belt as well. It didn't hurt much until I tried to lift my arm, and then it stabbed at me and my arm wouldn't go up any further.

Just for a minute I wished my ma was there, but I stopped that. I was on my own now. I swore and kicked the wall. It wasn't just the injuries that were pissing me off. It was the whole stupid mess I was in.

I found a puddle and washed the blood off my face. If I was with the lads, larking around, I would have left it there to look cool, but I didn't want anybody noticing me now. I walked in towards town for a while, but I didn't really know where I was going, or why, or what I would do when I got there.

I sat on a garden wall and took out my smokes. I had two left. I lit one of them. I should never have let Mick near that Skoda. I should have walked away from it when I had the chance. This was bigger trouble than I'd ever been in before. The cops would trace the car in no time and link it to me. Robbing a few quid or a phone was one thing. Robbing a car and driving to Dublin and crashing into another car and beating up the driver was something else altogether. They'd make room for me in St Pat's for that, no matter how crowded it was.

I had to think. I had to figure out what to do. There were some people waiting at a bus stop on the main road so I waited with them and tried to slip past the driver without paying. Some of them will let you away with it, especially if there's a few of you, because it's more trouble trying to get rid of you than it is to leave you on. But this fella wasn't having it. He turned off the engine and came back for me. I was cornered in the back of the bus and he was a big fella. I tried to get past him by jumping over the seats but my bad shoulder gave way and I cracked my jaw on the back of the seat. He grabbed me by the arm.

'Get off me!' I yelled at him. 'I'll have the law on you, you fucking pervert!'

'You just try,' he said.

He was Polish or something. Funny accent. I wriggled free and ran off the bus, and gave him the finger as he drove past. He gave me a big toothy grin, the faggot.

I walked on. At the next bus stop I thought of trying again, but I didn't have the energy. I was beginning to feel the lack of sleep and I was starving hungry as well.

I took out my phone and checked my credit. Three euros. I phoned Fluke but after a few rings it cut out, and when I tried again I got user unavailable. The bastard, my own cousin, had turned off his phone on me.

I tried Beetle again, but there was still no answer. I counted my money. I had the fiver I took from my ma plus about four euro in change. I could pay to get on a bus but if I did I couldn't buy fags and they were more important. So I walked all the way into the centre of town, and it's probably just as well I did because that gave me the chance to come up with a story.

19

My nine euro bought me a packet of smokes, a pint of milk and two bags of crisps. The paper shop was the only one open in the centre of town. It was too early for anything else. But the park was open in Stephen's Green so I took my stuff over there and lay down under a bush. I hardly put my head down before I was asleep.

My phone woke me a couple of hours later, but it was my ma so I didn't answer it. I went back to sleep, and the next time it rang it was Fluke.

'Where are you, you little wanker?' he said.

'I'm in town,' I said. 'And don't call me a wanker, you bollix.'

'You are a wanker,' he said. 'And the cops are looking for you. What happened last night?'

'Mick lost the plot,' I said.

'He lost more than that,' Fluke said. 'The guards caught him beating up some fella in Dalkey. He nearly killed him. Probably would have if they hadn't got there in time. And he was beside your Skoda.'

'He crashed it,' I said. 'And then when that other fella came over he went mental.'

'What were you thinking of?' he said. 'Why did you let him drive?'

'I couldn't stop him,' I said. 'And anyway, you let him drive.'

'Not when he's like that, I don't,' Fluke said. 'I don't go near him when he's like that. He'll get time for this, Bobser. He'll get two years at least. More if the fella dies.'

Good, I thought, but I didn't say it. 'And will he?' I said.

'He might. Punctured lung and head injuries. Mick went ballistic, they said. Why did you go robbing a fucking Skoda anyway? Heap of junk.'

'It was outside the door, that's why. And I came home, like I said I would.'

'Listen, Bobby,' he said, coming the older cousin all of a sudden. He did that sometimes. 'Your ma will never stick it down there. She'll do her head in with no one to talk to and that. Just give her a couple of weeks and she'll be back with her tail between her legs. That's what my ma says, anyway.'

'I don't care,' I said. 'I'm not going back.'

'Well what are you going to do then?'

'I don't know,' I said. 'I don't care.'

'My ma says you're to go to our place and she'll sort it out.'

'Sort what out?'

'With the guards and everything. And then you can get a bus back to Clare. Your ma's demented worrying about you.'

I hung up on him and turned off my phone. Two could play at that game.

My shoulder was worse – stiff and sore – and my head was aching. I was hungry again as well, but I was in no mood for robbing money. Not on my own. So I robbed a burger and chips off a woman outside Super-mac's and ran round the corner with them and ate them walking down Grafton Street under the noses of the guards there.

The headache kept getting worse. By the middle of the afternoon it was blinding me and I went into a pub and asked the bartender for an aspirin and a glass of water. He told me to fuck off so I picked up a stool and threw it over the counter and smashed all the bottles on his shelves for him. And then I ran again, dodging through the back streets and over the river and along to Moore Street.

But I was tired of running. It's different when you're with the others and it's like a game and you all think you're great, like in a war or something. It's not the same when you're on your own and you don't feel well. I half wished the guards would pick me up but they were all standing around in the streets, looking useless.

But I was happier on the Northside. It was different there. One of the street sellers gave me a couple of aspirin and a bag of bruised apples to wash them down with. I ate them walking up Dorset Street. I don't know where I thought I was headed, but my legs took me in that direction anyway, towards my own part of town. And then when I got to Drumcondra, the guards finally picked me up, and I got in the car without a word.

20

I knew the drill in the garda station. I'd been through it enough times. My ma was too far away to come in and I didn't give them Carmel's number. She was always giving out about me to my ma, and she'd be delighted to see me in here. But they weren't allowed to interview me without an adult there so they had to bring in a social worker. That took a bit of time to organize so they stuck me in a cell for an hour or two. I caught up on a bit more sleep, or at least, I tried to. Garda stations aren't the quietest places in the world.

When the social worker arrived her hair was all over the place like she had been out on her bike on a windy day. It didn't bother me. I'd seen this one before. She was often up around our flats. She would do fine.

There were two guards in the interview room. One of them I knew from another time when I was picked up. He sat through a long interview with me once when my ma was there. I never said a word the whole time. I knew what he thought of me but it was no harm that he knew my history. It might even help me with my plan.

The other guard was older. He was the one who did most of the talking. For the first while I played my old game, shrugging my shoulders and saying nothing. They asked me about the car and where I'd found it and why

I'd stolen it and where I got the key from and what time I left for Dublin and what time I got here and why I ran away. I gave them nothing, just stonewalled completely until the older one said: 'How long have you known Michael Kilroy?'

I squirmed in my chair and looked as uncomfortable as I could.

'He's a friend of yours, right?'

I shrugged and said, 'Where is he?'

'He's locked up,' he said.

'Here?'

'Never mind where,' he said. 'You don't have very good taste in friends, do you?'

I sat back in my chair and went back to stonewall mode.

'This is very serious, Robert. This isn't like stealing a phone or a handbag. Your friend Mick put a fella in hospital last night.'

I wriggled again and crossed my arms and uncrossed them again.

'He nearly killed him. Were you there? Did you see it happen?'

'No,' I said.

'Where were you then?'

'I ran away.'

'He's a very dangerous fella, your Mick,' he said. 'We don't often see damage like that inflicted on a person without the use of a weapon.'

'Will you put him away?' I said.

'You can bet your life we will,' he said.

'How long for?' I said.

'I'd lock him up for good if I had my way,' he said. 'But he'll probably get five or six years.'

I gripped the edges of my chair and tried to look worried. Then I nodded towards the social worker beside me.

'Can I talk to her? On my own, like?'

The two guards looked at each other and then they said I could. They turned off the tape recorder and went out and I said to the social worker, 'If I tell them about Mick will it get back to him?'

'I can ask them that,' she said.

'I won't give evidence,' I said, and I chewed at my fingernails. 'No way in the world I'm standing up in court. It's more than my life's worth.'

'I'll tell them that as well.'

She went outside and I screwed up my face to stop myself smiling. It was going great. Then they all trooped back in again.

I pointed at the tape recorder. 'I don't want that on,' I said.

'We have to turn it on,' the old guard said. 'But it's only relevant to your case and not to Michael Kilroy's.'

'You can't use it as evidence?'

'No.'

'Because I won't give evidence,' I said.

'We understand that.'

'You can't make me.'

'No. We can't,' he said.

I stopped and did some more wriggling around in my chair. They waited. Eventually I said: 'Mick . . . Mick made me do things.'

'What kind of things?'

'He made me rob stuff and that. Money. Phones. He had to feed his habit. I didn't dare say no to him.'

'Why not?'

'You've seen what he's like!' I said. 'He's a mentaller. He was scared of getting caught but he knew I wouldn't get sent down for stuff because I was too young. So he made me do all his dirty work for him. He threatened me with all kinds of stuff if I didn't do it. And then he'd buy drink and drugs and whatever he needed.'

'Where did he buy the drugs?'

'I don't know. Honest. I never bought any myself. I had to give him everything I robbed.'

'Did you steal anything else for him? Apart from phones and money?'

'Cars,' I said. 'Mick likes driving.'

'What cars? Where?'

I shook my head. 'I'm not saying. I don't even know why they took me with them most of the time.'

'Who's they? Are there more of them?'

I went silent. I'd gone a bit far there. I'd said more than I meant to.

'Your cousin Luke, is it?' the old guard said.

'No,' I said. 'I'm not saying. In any case the others

were never so bad. Mick was the worst. I been scared shitless of him for the last few years.'

I was dying to know if they were buying it or not but I didn't dare look them in the face. I just kept my head down and chewed at my nails.

'That was why my ma took me away down the country,' I said. 'I was always in trouble. And I couldn't sleep at night for fear of what Mick would do to me.'

'So why did you come back in such a hurry?' the other guard said. He sounded like he didn't believe me. 'And why did you meet up with Mick?'

'He made me!' I said. 'He told me I had to get a car and come back and work for him again or he'd—' I stopped.

'He'd what?' the old guard said.

I managed to squeeze a few tears from somewhere. 'He said he'd find us, wherever we went. He said he'd mess up my ma's face.'

21

It worked. I got a ten-mile-long lecture about what happened to lads like me if we didn't stick to the straight and narrow and how hard it was to get your life back on track if you got a bad start and how I was still young enough to change my ways and make a go of it and if I didn't it would be St Pat's for me next time and blah blah blah. I put up with it, and tried to look innocent and grateful, and I said I would make something of my life now Mick was out of the way and couldn't force me to work for him no more. Then they put me in a garda car and drove me down to my ma in Clare. I slept nearly all the way in the back. Best taxi service in the country.

They had a long talk with my ma when we got there and I heard most of it through the thin floor in my room. My ma kept saying, 'He's a good lad, really,' and 'There's no real harm in him,' and 'That's why I brought him down here.' Stupid cow. As if bringing me down here was going to change anything.

After they left I waited for my ma to tear into me like she usually does, but it didn't happen.

'I never knew that, Bobby,' she said. 'About Mick Kilroy. You should have told me. Why didn't you tell me?'

I shrugged and tried not to laugh.

'But he's gone now. He won't bother you no more,' she said. 'This is a new start now. Everything is going to be different.'

For a second I almost believed her. Then the hole where my future should have been gaped wide open again.

I wished I hadn't slept so much in the garda car. I lay awake for hours, listening to the night noises, inside and out. There were rats or bats or something in the roof, and every few minutes one of them went skittering across the boards above my head. I kept thinking about the little girl and how they murdered her. Did they strangle her? Stab her? I kept getting this picture of her, half cat, fighting for her life and screaming.

Something on soft feet went along beside the house and knocked into the ash-can. It must have been the dog, because I heard it come in through its flap and bump around in the kitchen, and then it went out again, and then I heard its claws on the kitchen floor and I wasn't sure whether it was in or out or whether I was awake or asleep, and then I dreamed that psycho Mick was out on bail and running at the back door with an axe.

22

I was out by the hayshed having a smoke when Coley Dooley landed in. He came across the fields and climbed over the wall behind the house.

'You're back,' he said.

'I am,' I said. 'Are you still allowed to talk to me?'

'Probably not,' he said. 'My father isn't too happy about the Skoda.'

'Why not?' I said. 'I moved it for him, didn't I?'

He laughed and looked back up towards his house.

'Why did you take it?' he said.

'I wanted it. Quickest way to get to Dublin.'

'Where is it now?'

'In the garda pound probably. My friend crashed it.'

'Did he?'

'Yeah,' I said. 'Then he kicked a fella half to death.'

He looked at me and I could tell he didn't believe me. I didn't blame him. Things like that didn't happen down here in fairyland.

'If you were so keen to go to Dublin why did you come back?' he said.

'I didn't want to,' I said. 'The guards brought me.'

'That's what Mrs Grogan's telling everyone,' he said. 'I didn't believe her.'

'Who's Mrs Grogan?'

'She lives in that yellow house on the way into the village. She sits beside the window all day long, watching who's going up the road and who's going down the road. She doesn't miss much.'

I lit another smoke and offered him one. He shook his head.

'Do you want to see the forts?'

'What forts?'

'The fairy forts.' He pointed across the road. 'One over there on Kevin Talty's land, and the other one behind you on that little hump. That one's on our land.'

I looked where he was pointing. I couldn't see much in either direction.

'This house was built between them. That's why it always had bad luck, according to my grandmother. That's why you have to put out the milk and a bit of cake for the fairies.'

'Cake?' I said. 'I don't remember anything about cake.'

He was laughing again. 'And a bit of roast chicken on Sundays,' he said.

'Fuck off!' I said, but I couldn't help laughing with him.

We went out the gate on to the road.

'Aren't you going to tell your mother where you're going?' he said, just like last time.

'No,' I said. 'Do you always tell your mother where you're going?'

'I do,' he said. 'Or my father. They want to know. Doesn't your mother want to know?'

'She can ring me if she wants me,' I said.

To me a fort was a place with walls and battlements and gun turrets. The ones Coley showed me were disappointing. They were just circles in the fields with a grassy bank and a few bushes.

'And?' I said to him.

He shrugged and laughed. 'I just thought I'd show you,' he said. 'So you'd know.'

'Know what?'

He laughed again. 'Where the fairies are supposed to live.'

We were standing in the first fort, the one on his land. It was on a useless-looking field over to the left of the two big meadows between my house and his. There was nothing much to see.

'There's supposed to be an old cave under there,' he said, showing me a muddy hole in the ground. 'And a tunnel. It comes out on the other side of the hill near the river.'

'What kind of a cave?' I said.

'My grandfather says it's big enough for you and me to stand up in. He used go down into it when he was a young lad. Do you want to go in?'

In my book that was a challenge, but I didn't like the look of that hole. It was just about big enough to crawl into but you'd have to lie down and slide in on your belly, head first into the darkness.

'Why not?' I said. 'After you.'

'No way,' he laughed. 'It's only badgers use it now. If you met one of them lads down there he'd take the face off you. Specially if he had pups.'

'He would not,' I said. There were badgers in my old videos that I used to watch when I was Dennis's age. They were furry and wise.

'He would,' he said. 'If you go out walking in the fields at night you have to put a stick down your trouser leg, because if a badger gets hold of you he won't let go until he hears the bone snap.'

'Bollix,' I said.

'Try it then,' he said. 'Go in backwards and let him have your feet.'

'I will,' I said. 'After you.'

We had to practically wade through mud to get to the other fort, past a cattle feeder where Kevin Talty's cows had ploughed the land with their feet.

'He isn't the best farmer in the world,' Coley said. 'By rights he ought to harrow this and level it off. But you didn't hear that from me.'

The other fort was pretty much the same as the first one, except the bank was a bit higher.

'There's supposed to be a cave under this one as well,' Coley said, 'but the way in is lost now.'

'Any treasure in them?' I said. 'Gold? Silver?'

'I wouldn't start digging in this one anyway,' he said. 'Kevin Talty wouldn't be too happy about that, and he has a fierce bad temper if you get on the wrong side of him.'

He looked at his watch. 'I'd better go back for my dinner,' he said.

'Can't you just have it when you want?' I said.

'I could.' He laughed. 'But I'd want a better excuse than this. My mother just sent me down to see if it was true, what Mrs Grogan saw.'

'Well it is,' I said. 'So you can run home and tell her.'

He nodded. 'Did you really crash the car?' he asked me.

'I didn't. My friend did.'

'How bad is it?'

'Side's bashed in. It's a write-off, I'd say.'

He thought about this for a minute. Then he said: 'My father thought you had just taken the car and hidden it down a borreen or something. Just a prank, like. He'll probably throw you all out, now.'

'Good!' I said. 'Exactly what I was hoping for.'

I expected him to laugh, but he didn't.

'You shouldn't have taken it,' he said.

'Why not?' I said. 'He wasn't using it.'

That was one of our big jokes, me and the lads. But Coley didn't find it funny.

'I'm not using my bike,' he said. 'Doesn't mean I don't need it.'

A fuse started to blow in my head.

'He's gone, isn't he? This Lars bloke? If he

wanted his car so badly why didn't he take it with him?'

'It doesn't matter,' Coley said. 'You shouldn't have taken the car. It didn't belong to you.'

He turned and walked away across the field. That was when I noticed he was wearing his wellies. I looked at my own feet. My trainers were filthy and soaked right through. I swore, and I nearly called out after him to tell him what I thought of him. *You shouldn't have taken it. It didn't belong to you.* He must have been soft in the head or something, to think life was as simple as that.

23

PJ Dooley called in on his way home from work. When I heard the knock on the door I legged it upstairs. My ma was watching TV with Dennis. I heard her tell him to stay where he was and not dare move, so she knew as well as I did there was trouble coming.

She went out and let PJ into the kitchen. I stood on the top step and listened. He didn't hang around to pass the time of day. He said: 'I'm sorry now, but I'll have to ask you to leave.'

'Oh, no,' my ma said. 'We can sort it out. I'll pay for the car. And I have your deposit, look.'

I knew where she kept her large notes. In an envelope inside her bra. I could see it in my mind's eye, what she was handing him. A crumpled brown envelope with one end slightly damp from being too near her armpit.

'The car didn't even belong to me,' said PJ. 'I have no way of claiming for the insurance on it or anything.'

'We'll pay for it,' my ma said, and I could hear that little husky squeak in her voice that always came along with the waterworks. 'We'll pay it in instalments. I'll give you the first one as soon as I get my dole.'

My ma's whole life was paid for in instalments. Clothes, the telly, the washing machine, birthdays,

Christmas, everything. Two different money-lenders came to the door every Friday morning. She never had enough to pay both of them, and the debts just kept getting bigger and bigger. I wondered what they would think when they found she'd moved out of the flat.

'You will have to pay for it,' PJ said. 'We'll have to see about doing it through the courts.'

'Oh no, please!' she said. She was in floods of tears now. 'Don't put us out. He's not a bad lad, honest he's not. Bobby!' It came out high and shrill. 'Get down here!'

I didn't move. PJ started to say something but she barged on straight over him.

'He got mixed up with the wrong kind of lads. Even the cops said that. He was being bullied by the fella that crashed your car. That's why I brought him down here. To get him away from them.'

'All the same,' PJ said, but she was yelling up the stairs to me. 'Bobby! Come down and tell Mr Dooley what happened!'

I held my breath.

'Look,' said my ma, and I heard her rustling a newspaper. She had showed me that earlier, after she came back from the village. There was a picture of the two cars up on the roundabout and a story about the fella who was beaten up.

'See?' she said. 'There's the car, see? And look what it says.'

She left PJ looking at it and flew up the stairs. I

backed into the bedroom but she came in after me, her face all blotchy with fury and tears. She knew better than to try and grab me. I'd hit her before, more than once.

'Please, Bobby!' she whispered.

'Fuck off!' I whispered back.

'Just tell him!'

'No way!' I said.

'All right,' she said. 'You can go to Dublin at the weekend if you tell him. I'll give you the bus fare.'

I had her now.

'Fifty quid,' I whispered.

She closed her eyes and took a deep breath, then she nodded. I had no idea why this place was so important to her. She went down and I followed her. PJ looked up from the newspaper.

'That's the car, isn't it, Bobby?' my ma said. 'This fella made Bobby steal it and bring it up to Dublin. He was making him do bad stuff for years, wasn't he?'

I nodded. Long face. My best victim look.

'That's why I moved down here,' my ma said. 'To get Bobby away from those lads. Bad influence. He's a good lad underneath it all, aren't you, Bobby?'

I kept my eyes down and my face straight.

'And that fella's in jail now,' she said. 'Mick Kilroy, his name is. They'll put him away for years after what he done. They said so, didn't they, Bobby?'

'They did,' I said.

'So he can't threaten him no more. Bobby needs

another chance. Even the guards said that, didn't they, Bobby?'

I nodded again.

'Please don't throw us out, Mr Dooley,' my ma said. 'It won't happen again, honest.'

PJ looked around the kitchen. My ma hadn't washed up since we got there. She never washed up until there was nothing left to eat off. There was half a tomato trodden into the floor and a big dirty splash of tea where I knocked over a cup. I was an idiot to agree to fifty euro. After all, I wanted to be thrown out, didn't I?

'I was just about to clean up,' said my ma. 'The water's on to heat.'

PJ said nothing. He seemed to be stuck to the floor. My ma helped him along. She pushed the soft brown envelope into his hand. He stood looking at it like he had no idea what it was.

'There's eight hundred there,' my ma said. 'Four hundred deposit and a month in advance. Is that all right?'

I looked at my ma. Where the hell had she got eight hundred euro from?

PJ stood still another moment and then he turned and looked at me.

'Do you really want another chance?' he said.

In all honesty I had no idea what he was talking about. The only second chance I wanted was another go at getting back to Dublin. Everybody was always on about second chances, but what did they mean? A second chance at what? And what was the first chance supposed to be, and how had I missed it?

But I nodded anyway, because I knew it was something I was supposed to want.

'Then this is what we'll do,' PJ said. 'I'll find out the book price for an eight-year-old Skoda. And you can come up and work for me on the farm until you have it paid off.'

My jaw dropped. My ma's jaw dropped, too. In the front room Dennis giggled at something on the TV, and I wanted to laugh, too.

'Doing what?' I said.

'Whatever needs doing,' he said. 'You can work with Coley. He'll show you.'

'He'd love to, wouldn't you, Bobby?' my ma said.

I stared at her.

'It's up to you,' PJ said. 'But we'll have to sort it out one way or another. You can't just get away with taking a car and wrecking it.'

I opened my mouth to say I never wrecked it, but my ma was in first. She was beaming with gratitude.

'He'll do it, Mr Dooley,' she said. 'And thanks a million!'

He left, taking the brown envelope with him. I turned to my ma and held out my hand.

'Fifty quid.'

'The weekend. I said you could have it at the weekend,' she said.

'You said I could have the bus fare at the weekend. I want the fifty quid now.'

'Well I haven't got it,' she said. 'You can have it when my dole comes through on Friday.'

'Thursday,' I said. 'You get your dole on Thursday.'

'Thursday then,' she said.

I grabbed her bag and opened her purse. There was a crumpled fiver and some loose change. I picked out the fiver.

'Leave that!' she said. 'That has to last me the week!'

There were three packets of fags in there as well. I never knew my ma to let herself go short. I took one and put it in my pocket.

'You little bastard!' she said.

I threw the whole lot on the floor. Coins and lipsticks and keys scattered everywhere.

'You should know,' I said, and I went out for a smoke.

24

That night Jimjam bunny forgot to wake Dennis and I woke to the sound of my ma screaming at him and the bedsprings screeching as she shook him. He was whimpering and sobbing and saying sorry, but sorry was never good enough for my ma, I gave up sorry five years ago.

She left Dennis sobbing away to himself and came into my room.

'The mattress is soaked,' she said. 'I forgot to put the cover on it.'

I could see the cover in my mind's eye, a yellow, stinking, plastic thing, lying in the corner of the sitting room under a pile of socks and T-shirts.

'He wasn't supposed to be sleeping with me!' my ma said. 'What am I going to do now?'

'Turn it over,' I said.

'It's gone all the way through,' she said. 'How can a fella that size have so much piss in him?'

All I wanted was to go back to sleep.

'Stay in here if you want,' I said. 'I'll sleep in the little room.'

I don't know what she did in the end. The next time I opened my eyes she was bumping around in the kitchen and Dennis was complaining about the eggs again. I turned over and pulled the duvet over my head. I couldn't face a day that had absolutely nothing in it at all for me to do. But I had to get up in the end, and it was every bit as bad as I expected. I wished I'd let PJ throw us out. I couldn't believe I'd been so stupid.

I was never so bored in my life. I set up the Xbox but I was even bored with that. I smoked half the fags I took from my ma. I wandered around inside and I wandered around outside, but nothing I did would make the clock move any faster. It just seemed to be stuck. More than anything I wanted to get off my head. It was way too long since I'd had a drink, and I had no gear of my own – it was always Beetle got that. Twenty times I made up my mind to get on the road and start hitching back to Dublin, and twenty times I changed it again.

I bent over backwards to keep out of my ma's way. I knew if she got across me there would be serious trouble, the mood I was in. So if she was inside I went out and when she went out to the village with Dennis I went in. And somehow I made it through to the end of the day without hitting her or Dennis. In the evening PJ phoned and said he'd be down for me the next morning. I thought again of trying to make a run for it, but I didn't know where to go. I felt trapped. If I'd had a gun I would have taken hostages and demanded a helicopter out of there.

I went to bed as soon as it was dark, but I couldn't sleep for ages. Just lay there listening to the fuzzy sound of the TV down below, and re-living the best times with the lads, and trying not to think about tomorrow.

But eventually I did go to sleep, and the next thing I knew Coley Dooley was banging on the front door.

His da was outside, waiting on the tractor. While I got dressed Coley boiled the kettle and washed out a cup and made me a tea bag and a peanut-butter sandwich. It wasn't until I was outside sitting on the trailer with Coley that I even stopped to think.

I was willing to bet Coley never tried to drink a cup of tea on a trailer. It bumped all over the place and the tea slopped all over my legs and burned my knees. More of it went on the floor than in my mouth. Coley, as usual, kept laughing. He looked like he'd been up for hours, scrubbing his rosy cheeks in the shower. I wondered why I'd come out with him, instead of telling him to fuck off and leave me alone. I'd just got up and gone out on some kind of automatic pilot. Like with Coley and his grandda that other day – going with the flow.

But at least I was going to get another go of the chainsaw. PJ had taken the day off from his office to get us started, and he drove us out to a patch of forest at the foot of the mountain. They let me have first go of the saw. Coley hauled trunks and branches over and PJ split the logs and tossed them on to the trailer. But I didn't last ten minutes with the saw. I loved using it and I didn't want to stop, but my bad shoulder just couldn't take it. The weight of the saw put too much strain on it and the vibrations sent shooting pains up into my neck.

I turned it off and put it down.

'I can't do it,' I said. 'I hurt my shoulder in the accident.'

They both looked at me. I knew what they were thinking.

'I did,' I said. 'And I cut my head.' I felt the place. The bump was nearly gone but the cut was still there, with a big, crusty scab.

'Feel it,' I said to Coley. 'Go on.'

His hands were big and square but his fingers were gentle. He made a face.

'I'll do that,' I said to PJ. 'What you're doing.'

He handed me the axe. I could tell he didn't want to give it to me. My shoulder still hurt but I was able to arrange things so I could take most of the weight of the axe in my right hand, and chucking the bits up in the trailer was no problem.

PJ took over the chainsaw, but every now and then he had to stop to take a call from the office. Coley acted like his secretary, minding the phone and stopping him when it rang because he couldn't hear it over the noise of the chainsaw. When that happened I would run out of bits to split, and then I would go over and help Coley haul timber, using just my good arm.

I don't know why I did that. I was always telling my ma I was too sick to go to school. I could have used the shoulder as an excuse to scab off, but it was a bit like with the lads, I suppose. You couldn't show scared or weak, like. You were up there with the men or you were nothing. I didn't want Coley to think I was a girl, even if I thought he was.

We had ham sandwiches and chocolate biscuits and hot tea from a flask for our break. By the time we stopped for dinner the trailer was nearly full.

'Many hands,' PJ said and he let me drive the tractor back along the forest track as far as the road. I said I knew how to drive it but it wasn't like a driving a car. There was no accelerator for one thing, just a rev lever on the steering column. He had to show me and he gave me a lecture on how to drive safely and it pissed me off. I hate being told things.

We had a massive dinner in Coley's ma's kitchen. Pork chops and carrots and mountains of spuds boiled in their skins. I can't stand watching people eat but Margaret Dooley hardly took her eyes off me the whole time.

'Growing lad,' she said one time when I looked up and caught her at it. 'Sure, he's skinny as a whippet, would you look at him?' And every time after that I caught her looking she would just smile and push something at me. Butter, or bread, or more spuds.

Then there was apple tart and pots of tea and more choccy bikkies. Margaret washed every plate and cup and spoon as it came off the table. I never once seen a dirty dish in her kitchen. No wonder PJ had looked sideways at my ma's one.

I could hardly move after all that food, but we had to go and unload the firewood. I threw it off the trailer and the other two stacked it neatly in the end bay of the lean-to. I was finished way before they were, so when they weren't looking I sneaked off behind the buildings for a smoke.

I thought they might come looking for me but they didn't. I heard the regular thud and click of the wood-stack and the mumbling of their voices. When I finished my smoke I thought of going home. They couldn't keep me here. They couldn't make me work. There were laws against slave labour. But what would I do at home? Watch the afternoon soaps with my ma? Listen to her whinging on about how useless I was? Wait for them to come and get me again?

I thought of thumbing to Ennis and trying to rob a car and get back to Dublin. But if I messed up I was in serious trouble. Whatever else I did I had to keep my nose out of the garda station, for a while at least. I knew some lads who had been to St Pat's. Mick had been there for six months when he was fourteen, and he always laughed about it and said it was like a hotel and the other lads were great craic and had loads of good tips. But I couldn't see myself locked away and not able to get out, no matter what the other fellas were like. I'd go mental.

Maybe that was what went wrong with Mick.

The best plan, as far as I could make out, was to wait until the weekend and get the fifty euro from my ma and get up to Dublin and then stay there. Disappear. That would sort everything. Then PJ would throw her out of the house and she would have to go back and get another flat and everything would be back to normal again. No Mick, OK, but I still had Beetle and Fluke, and there were other lads from the flats and from school, so we could get someone else to join us if we needed to.

On my way back to the others I went in to look at the Land Rover. The bonnet was open and I leaned in. There was a greasy old blanket thrown in over the top of the engine, like there had been an accident or something. I looked behind me and then lifted one edge. Not an accident, maybe, but an operation. There were bits everywhere, springs and bolts and big chunks of metal with peculiar shapes. I didn't know what an engine was supposed to look like. I thought it was a kind of grey metal brain that told the wheels to move. But if this was a brain, it had burst.

'I wouldn't try stealing that,' Coley said, coming up behind me.

'I wasn't going to,' I said.

'You wouldn't get far in it,' he said, laughing. 'The cylinder head is off it.'

'Oh.' I shrugged, trying to look like I knew what he was talking about.

'Matty's waiting on a new head gasket. He says he's ordered it, but I don't believe him. He says he ordered it three weeks ago.'

He turned away and showed me another car.

'Vintage Mini,' he said. 'Nineteen-sixty-nine. Great body on it. Hardly any rust. Worth a few bob. But the engine is completely useless. Needs a transplant. Matty's waiting for a suitable donor.'

He pointed to a third car. 'And that's an old Merc. Does about twenty gallons to the mile. He wants—'

His father called him then, and he was already up in the cab of the tractor. Me and Coley climbed up into the trailer and we set off for the woods again, for another load.

25

After the second load PJ dropped me home in the car. It was about four o'clock, so we hadn't done a full day's work, but it was more than enough for me and I suppose he could see that. He said to my ma: 'He's not a bad lad. He'll soon get fit.'

I dropped into an armchair and rested my head on the back of it. I was exhausted, and aching from head to foot.

'Did you hear that?' my ma said, wading in through Dennis's Lego. 'He said you were a good worker.'

He didn't say that. I wished my ma would shut up. I knew that the next thing that came out of her mouth would be the wrong thing, and it was.

'Amazing, isn't it? I never thought you had it in you to be a farmer.'

I turned on her. 'I'm not a fucking farmer, all right? It's just slave labour, that's all. And it wasn't even his fucking car I took!'

I heaved myself out of the chair and pushed past her. I kicked Dennis's Lego house to bits on my way out. In my bedroom I lit a fag. I didn't care if she caught me. What could she do to me anyway? I finished it and chucked it out the window, then lay down on the bed, just for a minute, to rest my aching bones.

*   *   *

I woke at about ten o'clock. My ma was where she always was but she'd got Dennis off to sleep early. I don't know what bed he was in.

'Make yourself a sandwich,' she said. 'And make me a cup of tea while you're at it.'

My hands were all skinned and scratched and sore. There were dirty sticky bits all over them from the goo that comes out of the pine trees. I could still smell it on them. I tried to wash it off with washing-up liquid but the water was cold and the sink was full of dishes and the scrubber was buried underneath them somewhere. I dried my hands on a dishcloth and made the sandwiches and tea.

'Would you ever do the washing up, you slag?' I said to my ma.

'I'll do it tomorrow,' she said. 'I been too busy.'

'Too busy doing what?' I said.

'You should try minding Dennis some time,' she said. 'And in any case I'm exhausted. He's up nearly every night sleepwalking.'

'Sleepwalking?' I said.

'He keeps having these stupid dreams about a little fairy woman. He's driving me mental.'

I took my tea and sandwich back up with me and lay down on top of the bed.

When I next woke it was dark, and there was just the light from the landing squeezing under my door. I could hear someone moving around downstairs in the kitchen. There was a voice, talking in a kind of high-pitched whisper. Dennis.

Jimjam bunny was on the ball tonight, then. But who was he talking to? Was there another voice, whispering as well? My ma?

I turned over, hurt my bad shoulder, turned back again. The fridge door closed. More whispering. My ma never whispered. She never cared who she woke up. I yawned and realized I needed to piss. There was a duvet on top of me as well as underneath me. It was Dennis's one from his bed. My ma must have put it over me. I looked at my phone. It was three o'clock.

I heard the squeak of a cupboard door, a rattle of crocks, the clunk of something being put down on the table. A quiet, excited giggle from Dennis.

I sat up, and groaned with the pain and stiffness in my shoulders and back. I got myself carefully out of bed and went across the floor. When I opened my bedroom door I heard the dog flap swing closed and bounce a couple of times against its frame.

'Dennis?' I called.

He didn't answer. Down in the kitchen I seen that little green bowl out on the table, and a carton of milk and a packet of biscuits.

'What are you doing?' I said.

'Shh!' he said. 'The little woman is here.'

He knelt down in front of the dog flap and stuck his head out of it.

'Come back!' he called out. 'It's only Bobby.'

The rest of him squirmed out through the hole and the flap dropped behind him.

'Dennis!' I said. 'Get back in here, you little head-banger!'

I heard his bare feet on the concrete, running a few steps, and his little excited squeak. I reached for the door key but then I stopped. What if there really was something out there? The ghost of a murdered child who cried like a strangled cat? Mick and the axe?

I turned the key and opened it and went out. The darkness blinded me, but then it softened a bit and I could see Dennis standing on the edge of the grass with his back to me.

'Come back in!' I said to him. 'Do you hear me?'

He turned round and danced back to me. 'She went under the hedge,' he said, 'and out the other side.'

I reached for him and swung him up on to my hip, wincing at the pains all over me. He wriggled and looked back over my shoulder when I carried him indoors.

I said, 'Go to the toilet or my ma will throw Jimjam bunny in the fire.'

I put him down and he ran off. I was locking the back door again when I heard my ma coming down the stairs. She had that undead look that the sleeping pills always gave her.

'What you doing?' she said.

'Nothing,' I said. 'Dennis had a dream.'

'What's that thing doing there?' she said, pointing at the little green dish.

'He's just playing,' I said.

'In the middle of the night?'

'Well I don't know, do I?' I said.

She put the milk away. Dennis flushed the toilet and came out, wiping his hands on his pyjamas.

'What you been up to?' she said to him.

'I seen the little woman,' he said. 'She came in for her milk.'

'Not that again,' said my ma.

Dennis looked anxiously into her face, trying to judge her mood.

'She had a blue dress,' he said. 'Way down to here!' He touched the floor beside his feet. My ma seen the mud on them.

'Did he go out the door?' she said to me.

'Out the dog hole,' I said. 'He's OK, Ma. Leave him alone.'

'You're not to do that again, Dennis,' she said. 'Do you hear me? You're not to go out in the night. Go back up to bed now.'

He scooted past her and galloped up the stairs on all fours.

'Are you sleeping in that wet bed?' I asked her.

'I put the plastic cover on it,' she said. 'It doesn't come through.'

'Oh, yuck!' I said. I could imagine the wet mattress, festering underneath her.

'I'll buy them a new mattress,' she said. 'Just as soon as I get the money. I'm going to join the Credit Union in the village.'

'I hope they know what they're letting themselves in for,' I said.

26

I'd gone to bed so early that I was awake before eight o'clock. I was going to try and sleep some more, but then I remembered the hot tea burning my knees in the trailer. I didn't want that to happen again.

My jeans were filthy, all stained with the spilled tea and the pine resin and mud and everything. I badly needed some washing done. There was a bin bag full of dirty clothes that I'd brought down from Dublin, and I took it downstairs with me and emptied it on the porch floor in front of the bathroom so my ma couldn't ignore it.

It was nice being up early and on my own. Even Dennis wasn't up yet. The house was completely silent, with no rustles or creaks, like the ghosts had all vanished with the daylight. And the sun was out and the sky was clear blue. You notice things like that in the country the way you never do in the city. I was almost happy for a minute, but I caught myself in time and remembered how much I hated it here and how everything that mattered to me was behind me, back in Dublin.

It wasn't Coley who called for me this time. It was PJ. I didn't like that. Coley wasn't in the car, neither. I asked where he was. PJ wouldn't tell me until I got in.

'He's in Ennis. He works three days a week in the

supermarket. He doesn't start till eleven but he got a lift in with his brother.'

'Grease-monkey Matty?' I said.

He laughed. 'No. Desmond. He was just passing through and he stayed over.'

'How many brothers does he have?'

'Four. And two sisters.'

He began to list them all off, then. Which one was in the hotel business and which one was in Australia, but I just looked out the window and switched off. He was still talking when we pulled up outside the house.

'Right,' he said. 'We'll be cutting hay today. It's promised fine until the weekend.' He started across the yard and I followed him. 'We get contractors in to make the silage but I always like to make a bit of hay for the calves. They do better on it.'

He led the way into the machinery bay beside the hayshed. 'We can't cut the grass until the dew's off it, so we might as well give the mower a bit of a service.'

My job was to undo the blades from the old bar mower, one by one, and clean the dried grass and mud off them.

'It's an antique, really,' PJ said. 'No one uses these old things now. But it's still working, so why bother getting a new one?' He gave me a socket wrench and a paint scraper. Nuts and bolts again. I didn't mind this.

When I unscrewed the nuts and washers I put them in the zip pocket of my jacket. I seen PJ watching me.

'I'm not robbing them,' I said.

'I know you're not,' he said. 'It's a good place to put them. I'm forever losing the fecking things.'

The blades were heavy. After I'd cleaned one with the paint scraper I handed it to PJ and he went at the chipped edges with a file, working nineteen to the dozen, putting his back into it, working up a sweat. When he had finished with them they were sharp, but not sharp like the axe. You couldn't shave yourself with them. They weren't supposed to be that sharp. When they were all done we greased them and bolted them back onto the bar.

It took us about an hour and a half, but I never felt the time passing. Then it took us another hour or so to take the hay shaker to bits and clean and grease the drums and re-bend some of the wonky tines. And after that it was into the house for more of Margaret's hot, strong tea and ham sandwiches. I wondered how many pigs that family ate in a year.

PJ drove the tractor down to the hay meadow. I stood behind him in the cab and leaned on the wheel arch. When we got there he gave me a rake with a yellow plastic head and told me to come along behind him and pull the cut grass clear of the long stuff.

'Just on the first go round,' he said. 'After that there's no need.'

I'd been happier about my shoulder when we were working on the machines. Once the stiffness from the morning had gone out of it, it felt a lot better. But it was useless for this job. The pull of the rake hurt it and after a few minutes I had to try and do it with one hand. I was getting nowhere fast. PJ stopped the tractor and called me over.

'The shoulder still at you?' he said. 'Hop up here.'

He stood up out of the driver's seat and I got into it. He showed me how to raise and lower the mower and how to start and stop it. He stood beside me for a lap and a half of the field, correcting my steering a bit to begin with, then leaving it to me when I got the hang of the widths and distances. Then he told me to stop, and he got off and finished the raking while I carried on mowing on my own. When he had been all the way round, with one or two breaks to answer the phone, he flagged me down again.

'You're very good for a beginner,' he said.

'I've done a lot of driving,' I said.

'I'd say you have,' he said, 'but even so you picked this up very quick. Nice straight lines. Very accurate.'

I hid a smile. He had no idea of the kind of stuff we got up to in Dublin. The narrow alleys we went through. The footpath corners between shops and parked cars. One time I went through a gap between two garda cars. It was so tight I left both wing mirrors on the ground for them, but there wasn't a scratch on the paint-work when we set fire to that car.

PJ looked at his watch, and then he looked me in the eye.

'Can I trust you?' he said.

What kind of a stupid question was that? I'd rob him blind if I got half a chance.

'To do what?' I said.

'To finish mowing this meadow and then go in and do the next one in the same way. Starting on the outside like we did with this one?'

I shrugged. 'Yeah, I don't mind,' I said. 'I can do that.'

'Good,' he said. 'I have to go and talk to a fella about getting my baler fixed. He's had it all year.'

We swapped mobile numbers and then he said: 'No messing around now, you hear?'

I started the engine and engaged the mower. What did he mean by that? What kind of messing around could I do on a tractor? I could just see myself turning up at Fluke's place.

'Hey, Fluke, guess what? I got wheels.'

I could just see his face.

But I didn't mind doing the mowing. It was different, anyway. And what else was I going to do between now and the weekend?

27

I had another massive feed in Margaret's kitchen and then I mowed two little meadows on the other side of the hill. Then PJ showed me how to take off the mower and put the shaker on, and I went back and shook out all the hay I'd cut. PJ came and went, or stood by the gate and talked on the phone. Except on the roads I did every bit of the driving. I pranged the shaker once on a gate post but he said not to worry about it – things like that happened all the time.

When we were finished for the day he gave me a lift home. In the car outside the house he gave me a tenner.

'What's that for?' I said. 'I thought you were keeping my money for the car.'

'I am,' he said. 'That's a bonus. And any other day you work as hard as you did today I'll give you another one.'

He came into the house with me to talk to my ma. I was delighted to see she'd finally done the washing up, and she'd washed my clothes and all, and they were in a clothes basket on the kitchen floor.

PJ told my ma the book price on the Skoda was two thousand, one hundred euro, and I could work it off at fifty euro a day. If Lars hadn't turned up by the time it was all paid off he would give the money to his mother.

'Does she live around here?' my ma said.

'No,' PJ said. 'She lives in Sweden, but I'm in contact with her. She came over with her daughter to try and find out what happened to Lars. That was a good while ago. A few weeks after he left.'

'Did she find out anything?'

'No,' PJ said. 'She got the guards to ask a few questions around the place but they weren't really interested. They said it happens sometimes. People just suddenly decide to change their lives and up sticks. They usually turn up in the end. They had another look in the house but they didn't find his passport or his driving licence or his bank cards or anything, so he must have taken them with him. They said he could be anywhere.'

'It's a bit weird, isn't it?' my ma said. 'I hope nothing happened to him.'

'Ah, you'd know in a place like this,' PJ said. 'It's very quiet around here. Very safe.'

After he left my ma said to me, 'How long will it take you to work off two thousand, one hundred euro at fifty euro a day?'

'I don't know,' I said. I could have worked it out but what was the point? I had no intention of staying around to do it. 'Have you got my fifty euro?'

'No,' my ma said. 'How could I get your fifty euro? There's no bank machine in the village.'

'How are you going to get it, then?' I said.

'I have to go into Ennis tomorrow,' she said. 'I have to see about signing on down here. But I can't go until

the afternoon. I have to go to a funeral in the morning.'
She seemed delighted by the idea.

'A funeral?' I said. 'Whose funeral? You don't even know anyone around here. How could you be going to a funeral?'

'It doesn't matter whether you know them or not,' she said. 'It's different down the country. Everybody goes. It's a community thing.'

'You're off your head,' I told her. 'No way you have to go to it.'

'Well I want to,' she said. 'I like funerals.'

'How could you like funerals?' I said.

'They make me think,' she said. 'And anyway, I like the incense and the flowers.'

I remembered now. Sometimes when we went to mass in Dublin, me in my smart suit, there would be a funeral. Incense swinging over the coffin. Dust to dust. Ashes to ashes. I don't think I really knew what was going on in those days.

'Well, you better have my fifty euro for me when I come home,' I said. 'You just better.'

I don't know what bed Dennis slept in that night or whether he went to the toilet or had another tea party with his little friend. I slept like the dead and woke to the sound of my ma banging around in the kitchen. I thought I'd overslept and got up quickly and pulled on my filthy jeans. But she was just up early, still in her purple dressing gown, and she had the ironing board out again.

'Are my clothes dry?' I said.

'They're hanging on the line in the hayshed,' she said. 'You'll have them for tomorrow.'

I looked at the skirt she was ironing. 'You can't wear that,' I said.

'Is it too short?'

She began hunting through the pile on the table. I made tea and put on some toast.

'I could wear my green dress, I suppose,' she said. 'Would that be better?'

She ran upstairs to get it but I wondered why I'd bothered. She would still get herself up like a tart. Too much make-up. A couple of strands of her hair hanging down over her eyes and sticking to her bright red lipstick. She knew no different. I shoved the clothes off the table on to the floor and sat down to drink my tea and wait for my toast. It had just popped up when Coley arrived at the door.

There were just the two of us that day because PJ had to show someone round a couple of houses and then go to the funeral and after that he had to go and catch up on things in the office. We had to wait for the dew again and we were supposed to tidy up the yard while we were waiting, but it was pretty tidy to begin with so mostly we just messed around and told each other stories.

Some of mine shocked him a bit and the worst ones wiped the grin off his face for a while, but some of his were pretty gory as well. Like the bull that killed his six-year-old cousin and the fella down the road who lost his leg in a tractor accident. Margaret was out at the funeral so we made our own tea and ham sandwiches. Coley washed up afterwards and dried all the dishes and put them away. I would never have believed it if I hadn't seen it with my own eyes. How could a big fella like that be such a wuss? I couldn't watch him without bursting my shite laughing at him, so I went out and had a smoke while I was waiting for him to finish.

Coley wasn't old enough to drive the tractor on the roads but he did anyway. He said he had to sometimes because his da couldn't be coming home from work to drive a quarter of a mile and there was no traffic on those roads anyway, and all the local lads did it. I said it was disgraceful and that I was going to turn him in to the guards. He laughed but I just shook my head.

'The law's the law,' I said. 'The law's the law.'

It was an easy day. One of us drove the tractor with the shaker and the other one went along with the rake to pull wet bits out of the ruts where the shaker couldn't get to them. My shoulder was much better and I could manage that now, as long as I didn't let the rake get snagged in the grass. The sun was so hot and the hay was drying so fast that we turned it all twice, once in the morning and then again in the afternoon. Coley said his da wanted me over the weekend as well to help put it into windrows and bale it, but I said he was out of luck.

'Matty will have to help then,' Coley said. 'He won't like that.' And he laughed.

*   *   *

My ma was in great humour when I got home and I said
I wished there was a funeral every day and she said so
did she. I made her give me the bus fare as well as the
fifty euro and she said it wasn't part of the deal but she
knew it was and she gave it me anyway and there wasn't
even a row about it. But later on that evening her mood
changed. She got a phone call from her sister and they
had a huge screaming match with my ma storming
round the house crying and slamming doors and swearing at Carmel like she was in the room with her. I never
asked her what it was about. Me and Dennis watched
the telly and pretended it wasn't happening. When the
ads came on he said: 'Bobby?'

I said, 'What?'

'She has no mammy or daddy.'

I was only half listening. I was watching an ad for
my favourite kind of cider. 'Who has no mammy or
daddy?'

'The little woman,' he said. 'She lives all on her
own. It's because she's old and they're dead now.'

'Dennis,' I said. 'Do you know the difference
between waking up and dreaming?'

He thought about that for a minute, then he said, 'I
dreamed Mammy was dead, but she isn't, is she?'

She wasn't. She finished abusing Carmel on the
phone and came in to sit on the sofa and bawl her eyes
out. I didn't care what time it was. I went to bed.

*   *   *

My arms and face were a bit burned from all that sun but I slept well anyway and I got up early. I was in such a hurry to get out the door and start thumbing to Ennis that I was nearly at the village before I realized what I'd seen on the kitchen table.

That little green bowl again, lined with a filmy white coating of milk.

28

I was bored to tears on the bus and I kept thinking about all the iPods I'd robbed and wondering why I'd never kept one for myself. I never thought about it, I suppose. I just handed all that stuff over and drank or smoked what we got on the back of them.

So I made it a priority, and within an hour of getting to Dublin I had one. Another silly slapper fiddling with it in the middle of the street. They never learn. I got the headphones and all – ripped them right out of her ears – and I was gone before she knew what was happening. It was nearly too easy.

I walked along O'Connell Street, feeling on top of the world. I had sixty-five euros, the sun was shining and the whole city of Dublin was mine. I was home, where I belonged. I bought a tenner of credit and sat on a bench and put it into my phone. Then I rang Fluke.

'Where are you?' he said.

'I'm in town,' I said. 'My ma sent me up on the bus.'

'Did she send money for my ma?'

'No. What money?' I said.

'She owes her,' Fluke said. 'We had her money-lender around. My ma had to give him forty euro to get rid of him.'

'Well I haven't got it,' I said. 'She never said

anything to me about it. Why don't you come into town and we'll get it for your ma?'

'Fuck off,' he said. 'You're too conspicuous. And anyway, I'm moving today.'

'Moving where?' I said, but he had hung up on me, the bastard.

I didn't need him, anyway. I rang Beetle. This time he answered.

'Howya Bobser,' he said.

'Brilliant,' I said. 'I'm in town. You coming in?'

'Ah, I'm sick,' he said. 'My head's lifting. Have you got any money?'

'A bit,' I said.

'Hey!' he said. 'Roberto! Come up to the flat. I know where we can score some brilliant gear.'

I walked out to Beetle's place. We bought a half-bottle of vodka and a couple of cans of Red Bull then got the bus out to Coolock where his dealer lived in a house with fifteen deadbolts on the door. He had to ring him from across the road and give him a password, then wait. After a while a little kid came along. He only looked about nine. Beetle had to give him the password again and then the money – thirty euro – and then he went off. We waited again, and it seemed like ages. I thought he had just pissed off with the money, but eventually he came back again with the deal, and me and Beetle went off to the park to share it.

I hadn't been out of my head for ages and it felt

brilliant. The best thing about using is that you don't have to kill time. It just passes, so sweetly. Like it's killing itself. All your troubles disappear. There's no past and no future and nothing in the world to worry about. My ma and her money-lenders floated away like ghosts. My school collapsed in a heap of dust. The guards danced a set on O'Connell Bridge. I laughed and laughed and laughed.

Beetle lay on his back on the grass and laughed and said, 'Oh Jaysus. Oh Mary. Oh Joseph.' I lit a fag and made smoke patterns in the air with it, and I was enjoying that so much I completely forgot to smoke it and it burned right down to the filter. So I lit another one and smoked that, and it was so nice that I smoked another one, and then another, and then we started in on the vodka.

Time does funny things when you're out of it. I thought I only smoked those three fags but next time I looked my packet was empty and there was eleven in it when I got off the bus. I kept looking again, and then I turned the packet inside out in case they were hiding in there somewhere.

The sun was still out but I felt cold. I knew I was starting to come down. Already. And I was absolutely starving. Hungry enough to eat my two hands. Beetle was asleep beside the empty vodka bottle and I left him there. Good gear was wasted on him. What was the point of getting off your head if you just went to sleep? He could have my ma's sleeping pills for that. But I must have been asleep for part of the time as well. When I seen a clock it said six o'clock, and there was no way I'd been making smoke patterns for all that time.

I had to have chips. I still had a fiver and a couple of coins. There was a newsagent on the corner of the park. I wanted fags, but I had to have chips and I hadn't enough money for both. I went on till I found a chipper. The fella behind the counter gave me a funny look and he made me hand over my fiver before he would bag up my chips. I made him open them again and put on more salt and vinegar. He was mean with it, the wanker. But he called after me to take my change, so he wasn't that bad. I would have gone without it.

I leaned against the chipper window and swallowed my chips so fast they took the skin off my mouth. Then I threw up, and it felt like they burned me again on the way back. I didn't feel good at all. The street wouldn't stay still and I wasn't sure where I was. I was freezing cold and I kept pulling at my jacket and feeling in the pockets for the red hat my ma used to put on me in the pram. An old woman asked me if I was all right and I told her to fuck off. I grabbed a fella by the arm and asked him for a fag. He gave me the one he was smoking to get rid of me. It made me feel worse. I threw it in the window of a passing car. The fella jammed on the brakes and got out but when he seen me standing there laughing he got back in and drove away.

I sat on a plastic seat in a bus stop and put my head

down on my knees. This high-pitched sound started up and at first I thought it was a siren, and then I realized it was that creepy little girl with the high voice and she had followed me up from Clare. I stood up and looked around. I couldn't see her, but I knew she was there, dead or not.

I started walking. I never seen her but I knew she followed me because I kept hearing her the whole time, high wailing with words in it, but I couldn't make out the words. I started running, trying to get away from her. And the next thing I remember I was standing outside my ma's flat and banging on the door. A strange woman opened it.

'Where's my ma?' I said.

'I don't know who your ma is,' she said. 'Clear off.'

So I went a few blocks over, to Fluke's. Carmel opened the door.

'What are you doing here?' she said.

'My ma let me,' I said. 'She gave me the bus fare.'

'Did she send money for me?'

'No.'

'Then what you doing here?'

I shrugged. 'Where am I supposed to go?'

'Well you can't come in here,' she said. 'I'm going out with the girls and I'm not leaving you here to wreck the place.'

'I won't wreck the place,' I said. 'Where's Fluke?'

'He's moved out,' she said. 'Now piss off!'

I just stood there and she sighed and shook her head and moved out of the way to let me in. I knew she would. She's my ma's sister, after all.

I'd only just got there in time, though. She really was going out.

'Get yourself something to eat,' she said. 'You can stay in Luke's room. But you keep your dirty little hands to yourself, you hear me? If I find one thing missing . . .'

'I won't touch anything,' I said.

She went off to get dressed. I took three fags out of her packet and put them in my pocket. I'd only just put the packet down when she burst back in and grabbed her fags and lighter off the table and her handbag off the chair, and took them all with her back to her room. But I felt too sick even to laugh.

She slammed the door behind her when she went and it sounded like an explosion in my head. I made myself a sandwich and sat in front of the TV for a while. But the sandwich made me feel sick and I couldn't follow any of the programmes on the TV, not even the football match, so I went off to bed in Fluke's room.

I don't know about him moving out. There was so much stuff thrown around in there that I could hardly find the bed. Some of it was mine, a few bin bags of stuff they were minding for me. But most of it was his stinky old trainers and jeans and underwear. I waded through it and pushed a load of stuff off the bed, and crawled in under the duvet. I went out like a light.

*   *   *

Women's voices woke me up, shrieking and roaring like lunatics. She'd brought the whole fecking hen party home with her. I groaned and turned over and pulled the cover over my head but it was no use. Something crashed in the kitchen and they all screamed laughing at whatever it was, and they just went on and on.

It used to be like that in my grandma's when I was small and me and my ma were living with her. I remembered lying awake in my ma's bed and the whole flat full of loud voices and slamming doors and things crashing in the hall and the kitchen. Sometimes there were rows and it sounded like they were killing each other. Sometimes, when they'd been out drinking together, they would laugh, like my aunt and her friends were laughing now. I don't remember which frightened me more, the fighting or that wild women's laughter.

I had to piss, which meant passing by the kitchen door. I held on for a while, but in the end there was no way out of it. I got up and tiptoed along the corridor. I made it to the bathroom but they caught me on the way back.

'Is this him?' one of them said. 'Is he your Catherine's boy?'

Another one said, 'Oh, isn't he gorgeous? Come in here till we get a look at you!'

The kitchen light was too bright. Underneath it their faces were like something out of a Stephen King movie. All running mascara and smudged lipstick. All the wrong colours for human skin. I bolted for the bed-room. I heard Carmel calling out after me.

'Be like that, you little bastard.' And then she said to the others, 'He's worse than any of them.'

High praise, that, coming from Fluke's ma. It gave me a nice warm glow.

29

'Scumbag!' said Fluke. 'Get out of my bed!'

'I thought you moved out,' I said, trying to make my eyes open.

'I did,' he said. 'I just came home to pick up some stuff.'

'Where've you moved to?' I said.

'In with my girlfriend,' he said. 'She's got her own place. She has two nippers.'

'Two nippers?' I said. 'Are you mental or what? Why would you move in with someone who has two nippers? You'd be better off staying with your ma.'

'But I can't have sex with my ma, can I?' he said.

'Why not?' I said. 'It never bothered her before.'

'You dirty little bastard!' He launched himself at me, laughing and swinging. I grabbed his fist and we wrestled on the bed and it was brilliant, just like the old days. I kept wrenching my shoulder but I never said anything or tried to stop him. It was worth the pain to be back in with Fluke again. We fought until one of the bed legs gave way and we both said, 'Whoops!' at exactly the same moment, and then we both laughed until we couldn't breathe. Then we sat on the edge of his banjaxed bed and he gave me one of his fags.

'I hear you're turning into a farmer,' he said.

'I am in my arse,' I said. 'I was only keeping my ma happy. I'm not going back there.'

'Well you're not staying here,' he said.

'Why not? You've moved out, haven't you?'

'Anyway,' he said. 'You'd want to watch yourself.'

'Why?'

'What have you been saying to the cops? They were around here the other day asking me questions about Mick.'

'Is Mick out?'

'No, he's not out,' he said. 'No way they'll give him bail after what he done. But it sounded to me from what the guards said like someone's been telling stories.'

'Oh, fuck the guards,' I said. 'Let's go into town, you and me. I'm dying for a bit of action.'

'No way I'm working with you any more, you little scumbag,' he said. 'Not when you've started dropping your friends in it. And anyway, I've my mot and her nippers to look after now.'

His ma came in then, holding on to the wall.

'What've you done to the bed?' she said. 'You little bollixes. I'll kill the pair of you!'

She made us fix the bed before she'd let us have breakfast. Fluke stacked old comics and school copies under it until it stopped rocking. Then he filled two bin bags with shoes and clothes and CDs, and dumped them in the hall.

His ma made us coffee and beans on toast.

'You piss off home now,' she said to me. 'And tell your ma if she doesn't send me up some cash for the money-lenders I'll tell them where she's moved to. They don't like people running out on them.'

'I can't go back,' I said.

'What do you mean, you can't go back?'

'I lost my ticket,' I said. 'And I've no money for another one.'

'Jesus, Mary and Joseph,' she said. 'What did the poor girl ever do to deserve you?'

Fluke laughed and she swung her hand at his ear but she didn't hit him. She knew better than that.

'How much is it down to Clare?'

It was fifteen euros one-way. I said, 'Twenty quid.'

She shook her head and swore, but she opened her purse and gave me two tenners.

'She can add that to what she owes me,' she said. 'And I'll need another forty before Friday morning. I'm not paying off her debts for her. I can't hardly pay my own!'

I bought a ten-quid deal off a lad I knew in the same block of flats and then twenty fags and a packet of skins in the corner shop. With my last couple of euro I got the bus into town. The sun was shining again. I don't know why I thought about it but I did. If it was still shining in Clare, they would be baling the hay I cut.

* * *

I skinned up a joint in the hallway of one of the flats in York Street and smoked it on a bench on Stephen's Green. I never felt like robbing stuff when I was stoned. It made me too paranoid. I felt like everyone was watching me all the time and knew exactly what I was thinking. But the dope gave me the munchies as well and I could only live with that for so long. When I couldn't stand it any more I stood at the entrance to the park and asked people for money.

'Have you got a few cents, missus? Ah, go on. Just a few cents.'

It took me half an hour to get enough for a bag of chips, and after that I smoked the other half of my dope and went to sleep in the sun. When I woke up I was hungry again, but not for chips or chocolate. It took me a while to figure out what it was I wanted, and when I did I phoned Beetle.

'Have you got any more of that stuff?' I said.

'No,' he said. 'But I can get it. Have you got money?'

'No,' I said. 'But I will have soon.'

'Roberto!' he said. 'That's what I like to hear.'

'Give me a couple of hours,' I said.

Grafton Street was still busy but I had no intention of working there. Too many guards around and nowhere to run. I needed some place where people had plenty of cash on them, but close to some quieter back streets with places to hide. I wasn't used to working on my own with no one to back me up. I had to be sure to get it right.

I was still feeling paranoid, but not half enough. I was standing outside the smoke shop opposite Trinity when two guards cornered me. I never even seen them coming. And one of them was the same lad who picked me up in Drumcondra last week.

'Hello, Robert,' he said. 'What are you doing here?'

'Minding my own business,' I said. 'Why don't you?'

He didn't like that but he let it pass. 'I thought you were supposed to be down in Clare?'

'I am. My ma let me up for the weekend. I'm just on my way now to get the bus back.'

'What time is the bus?'

I took a wild guess. 'Four o'clock.'

'Too bad,' he said. 'You missed it.'

I was surprised. I must have been asleep for longer than I thought.

'What time's the next one?' he said.

'I don't know,' I said. 'Maybe six o'clock.'

'Right,' he said. 'We'd better get you down to Busáras, then.' He got on to the radio.

Oh, fuck. I couldn't believe it. He was actually going to frogmarch me to the bus.

The car was along inside two minutes, and he got in the back with me, and they ran down the bus lanes all the way along the quays.

'How's your mother doing?' he said to me.

'She's all right,' I said. 'She's minding her own business.'

When we got to Busáras he got out with me and came into the station. There was a bus there waiting with Limerick on the front. You had to change there for Ennis. I hoped he didn't know that, but he did.

'There's your bus,' he said. 'Have you got your ticket?'

'No,' I said.

'You'd better get one, then.'

There were people lined up, getting on the bus already. I hoped it would go without me. I joined the queue at the ticket window. The guard stood in the middle of the station, watching me. When I got to the window I said, 'I lost my return ticket. Can I have another one?'

'Where you going?' the woman said.

'Ennis.'

'Fifteen euro,' she said.

'But I bought my ticket,' I said. 'I just lost it. I've already paid.'

'Nothing I can do about that,' she said. 'Fifteen euro to Ennis.'

'I haven't got fifteen euro,' I said. 'And I have to get back to Clare.'

'Can you move out of the way,' she said. 'There are people waiting.'

'Ah, please, missus,' I said. 'My ma's down there on her own. She needs me. She's scared being on her own.'

'It's fifteen euro for a ticket to Ennis,' she said.

I looked round. The cop was still there, fuck him. I

took the few cents I had left out of my pocket and dropped them in the metal tray.

'Please, missus!' I said. 'I'm desperate! I have to get home. I already paid!'

She pushed the money back at me.

'Clear off,' she said, 'or I'm calling the guards.'

I took the money and pretended to look at it like it was my ticket, then I put it in my pocket and gave my guard the thumbs-up. He nodded, but he still didn't go away.

I went over to the bus and got on. It was nearly full and just about to move off. I went straight past the driver and found an empty seat.

'Oi,' he said. 'Ticket.'

I got up and went halfway back along the bus. 'I lost it,' I said. 'I had a return but I lost it.'

'That's not my fault,' he said. 'You'll have to get another one.'

'Please, mister,' I said. 'I have to get down the country. I came up this morning. You seen me. You were driving.'

'I was in Dundalk this morning,' he said. 'Get off this bus, right now.'

'Please, mister,' I said. 'My ma needs me down in the house. She's sick. She's dying of cancer.'

He got up out of his seat and came down the bus to get me, but this old man in a seat just beside me nudged me on the arm.

'Here,' he said, and he handed me a twenty-euro

note. I stared at it, then at him, then I handed it to the bus driver. He didn't take it.

'You can't be paying for the likes of him,' he said to the old man.

'I can do what I like,' said the old man. 'He has the money now. Give him a ticket.'

The driver stopped to think about it. I knew he didn't want me on his bus at all. I nearly told him I didn't want to be there, neither, but I kept my mouth shut. It was better than more trouble in the garda station.

He took it in the end and went and printed me out a ticket, and gave me a fiver's change. I tried to give it back to the old man but he waved me away.

'Get yourself a cup of tea in Borris,' he said.

I did, when the bus stopped there, and a sandwich as well. Afterwards I stood and smoked a fag on the footpath and when the old man came past I offered him one.

'Ah no,' he said. 'I gave them up years ago.'

'Go on,' I said. 'One won't kill you.'

'No, no,' he said. 'You keep them.'

'I've loads of them,' I said. 'Go on. Take one.'

'All right, then,' he said. 'I'll put it behind my ear for later.'

That was all right. I didn't care what he did with it. He could throw it in the bin for all I cared. But he took it from me and that was what mattered. He let me give him something back for what he done for me.

30

I had to wait for an hour in Limerick and it was after eleven when I got off the bus in Ennis. There was no way I was going to thumb home in the dark. Our village was twenty kilometres out the road towards the coast and you wouldn't know what kind of redneck weirdos you'd get out there. And there was no way I was going to walk it, either.

I went into the centre of town and opened a taxi door. I told him where I was going and asked him how much. He just looked at me and said nothing. I turned on the charm.

'It's OK. My ma was supposed to collect me but the car broke down. She said to get a taxi and she'll pay you when we get there.'

'All right,' he said. 'But it'll cost forty euro.'

'That's OK,' I said, and jumped in.

When we got to the house the taxi driver followed me in. My ma heard us and came out of the sitting room.

'You owe him forty quid,' I told her, and ran up to my room, and listened to the argument from there. She didn't have forty euro. She never gave me permission. He didn't care if it was all she had for the week. He wasn't taking No for an answer.

I heard her spill out the contents of her purse on the

table and, for some reason, the sound gave me a little pain under my ribs.

'There's fifteen,' she said. Coins slid and chinked. 'Twenty. Twenty-three. That's all I've got. I'll have to give you the rest some other time.'

'I'll be back for it,' he said.

The front door slammed and then the taxi door, and the angry motor revved into the distance. I thought my ma would come up and I braced myself for a row.

But she didn't. I had to listen to her crying instead. I hated her for it. She did it on purpose, I knew, just to get at me.

31

The next morning, while we were waiting on the dew, PJ drove me and Coley into town with the small trailer attached to the back of the car. We went into a builders' supply yard and loaded up the trailer with unplaned timber, corrugated iron, drainage pipes and about a ton of cement.

'It's for a shed,' Coley told me. 'For my weanlings.'

'What's a weanling?' I said.

He laughed. 'A very small cow,' he said.

The rest of the day we were bringing in bales. My shoulder was miles better but it wasn't up to throwing bales up on to the big flat-bed trailer, so PJ showed me how to stack them so they wouldn't fall off and I did that job instead.

I was glad I did. Coley and his da were the strongest fellas I'd ever seen. We loaded the trailer six or seven bales high, and when we got near the top they had to throw them up higher than their heads. Higher even than their arms could stretch. I could never have done that. Some of those bales were still a bit damp and they weighed half a ton, but they kept on tossing them up to me like they were empty cardboard boxes.

PJ drove back to the yard and me and Coley rode

back on the top of the load. It kept swaying all over the place with all the bumps and potholes on the road.

'I hope you stacked them properly,' Coley said.

'Course I did,' I said.

Suddenly he jumped and sprawled full length and clawed at the bales for a hand-hold. Without thinking I grabbed his shirt at the shoulder, convinced that he was falling. But he was laughing, just messing. I wanted to hit him for making a fool of me, but he didn't even realize. He just kept laughing. He thought he was great. He didn't even notice that I didn't think he was funny at all.

In the hayshed we had to stack the bales up even higher. We did it in stages as each load came in, and left steps up all the way so they could climb up to throw the bales to the top. Even so, there were times when they had to use pitchforks to get the bales up to me. By the middle of the afternoon I was done in and my hands were all blistered and skinned from the string. PJ lent me leather gloves but it was already too late. I wanted to chuck it in and tell them to stuff their fucking bales, but I couldn't do it. They were like two machines, their muscles like big pistons. I couldn't cry off, even when my shoulder started paining me again. It would have made me look like a big girl's blouse.

So I gritted my teeth and kept going, and my blisters burst inside my gloves and my shoulder went through pain and out the other side, and I got some kind of weird second wind, almost like being stoned, so I worked in a hazy, dreamy space. One by one we gathered the loads from the fields and one by one we stacked them in the shed, and there were times, during all that, when I felt like I was a machine, too.

But when we finally finished and I took off the gloves PJ said, 'Mother of God. Look at the state of his hands!'

He made me wash them in warm, salty water, and then he gave me twenty euro and said, 'You're a great lad, God bless you. But you should have said something sooner.'

I walked back down home with Coley, swinging my raw fingers in the breeze.

'Does he pay you the same money?' I asked him.

'He doesn't pay me anything at all,' Coley said, 'but he's buying me six weanlings when I get the shed built and I'll make more out of them.'

'Very small cows,' I said. 'How can you make money out of very small cows?'

'They'll grow,' he said. 'And they'll turn into very big cows, God willing.'

My ma wasn't talking to me because of the taxi. It was another of the ways she had of getting at me. But I could always get around this one.

'Look at my hands,' I said.

She looked.

'It's from the bales,' I said. 'The inside of my gloves was sticking to them. They took half my skin with them when I pulled them off.'

She turned her back, putting dishes away. She'd washed up for the second time.

'You owe Carmel a hundred euro,' I said.

Silence.

'Eighty euro for the money-lender and twenty euro for my bus fare.'

'But I gave you your bus fare!' she said.

'I lost my ticket,' I said. 'I had to get another one.'

When she finished giving out to me about that, she got annoyed with PJ instead because of the state of my hands.

'He has no right to work you like that,' she said. 'You're not a donkey.'

'I know,' I said. 'It's not right.'

'And another thing,' she said. 'There's no cable for the DVD player. I told him and he says it's probably behind all that stuff under the stairs. He said not to bother dragging it all out and that he'd bring me another one, but he hasn't.'

'When did you ask him?' I said.

'Saturday.'

'Give him half a chance,' I said. 'It's only Monday.'

'I don't care for myself,' she said. 'But it's for Dennis. He's missing all his favourite films.'

'Why don't you get him outside?' I said. 'Take him for a walk or something.'

'I do,' she said. 'I take him down the shop with me nearly every day.'

* * *

She wasn't so worried about the state of my hands when she made me drag down the wet mattress an hour or so later.

'It'll never dry up there,' she said, and she was right. The whiff of it would make you want to throw up. We hauled it down the stairs and out the back door and draped it over an old wooden turf barrow we found in the shed. Then she got the hose out and sprayed it down until the water was running right through it and out the bottom.

'It'll dry out in a couple of days in this weather,' she said.

But when I looked at the sky I wasn't so sure. I could already see a band of dark cloud beginning to move in.

32

Something woke me. I thought it was something downstairs, inside the house, but then I heard the biffing of raindrops on the roof and I knew it was that. My first thought was that we got the hay in just in time. It made me laugh, and then I thought of Coley pretending to fall off the hay wagon and that made me laugh again. The stupid wanker.

And then I did hear something downstairs. Something sliding on the table. Or maybe it was the dog, knocking against the leg of it or something. I held my breath. Was someone whispering? I couldn't tell with the rain on the roof, and the run-off in the gutters was sort of whispering as well.

My ma was sleeping on the sofa in the sitting room. She said she wanted to because she liked the fire and she could go asleep watching the telly. She quite often did that anyway. But from in there she couldn't hear Dennis if he got up. There were two doors and the end of the porch between her and the kitchen.

The rain slackened off a bit. I could definitely hear whispering now. A high little voice. Dennis? It sounded too husky, like my ma when she'd been crying. Maybe it was only her, down there with Dennis. Except my ma never whispered.

There was another clunk. I leaned up on my elbows and my bed creaked. The sounds downstairs stopped.

'Dennis?' I called out.

The dog flap rattled. I jumped out of bed and ran down. I expected to find him outside again but he was in the middle of the kitchen, watching me with a scared look on his face.

'What you doing?' I asked him.

The little green bowl and a glass tumbler were out on the table, both half filled with milk. There was a Battenberg cake there as well with a few rough slices hacked off it and all the little pink and yellow cake squares picked out and piled up in a pyramid. Or not all of them, maybe. There were some pink and yellow crumbs on the table as well, soaking up spilled milk. I looked at the little eejit standing there in his pyjamas. He was terrified of me.

'Go to the toilet,' I told him. He ran in there and I threw the milk in the sink and wiped up the mess. I didn't know what to do with the cake. I ate a couple of the pink squares but I was never much gone on sweet things unless I was stoned, and I couldn't stand the marzipan from the outside. None of us could. I don't know why my ma bought that kind of cake. We always threw half of it away, anyway.

I held a stringy piece of marzipan over the dog's nose. It snapped and it was gone. I fed it the rest of the messy stuff, and then Dennis came back in.

'What were you up to in here?' I said to him.

'She wanted her milk,' he said.

'Who did?'

'The little woman.'

I grabbed him roughly by the arms and bent down to look him in the eye.

'Listen to me,' I hissed at him. 'I've had enough of you and your little woman. When I go to bed I want to sleep, right? I don't want to be woken up by your stupid little tea parties. Got it?'

He nodded. His eyes were wide and frightened. 'Where's Mammy?' he said.

'She's asleep,' I said, 'and she's staying that way.'

I swung him up on to my hip, then I turned out the light and carried him upstairs.

'I want Mammy,' he said. 'I want to go in Mammy's bed.'

'She hasn't got a bed,' I said. 'You pissed in it, remember?'

I dumped him in his own bed and pulled the duvet up over him, then went back to my own room. Dennis whinged to himself for a while, but he knew better than to cry too loud. It was the same with me when I was little. My ma hated being woken by crying. You had to wheedle your way around her to get what you needed or else you would go without. Crying only ever got you a slap.

He went quiet after a while but I still couldn't sleep. I was listening and listening. But the rain had stopped and the rats were asleep or out, and the countryside all around was as silent as the grave.

33

It was raining again in the morning but it wasn't as bad as it looked once I got out in it. It wasn't cold. Coley came down on his bike and let me slow-pedal it back while he walked along beside me.

'Why don't you get one?' he said.

'I will,' I said, 'if you leave it outside your house some night.'

He laughed. 'No chance. That cost me three hundred and fifty euro.'

'They saw you coming,' I said, looking down at it. 'Where did you get three hundred and fifty euro?'

'I got nearly two thousand,' he said. 'This Easter. I sold my two best bullocks.'

'That must have been sore,' I said. 'Will they grow back?'

The bullock jokes lasted all day while we worked on Coley's shed. There were two of them, actually, built side by side in a grassy hollow behind the main farm buildings. They were in ruins – nothing left except for broken walls and a few rotten roof beams.

'Do you know how to fix them?' I asked him.

'Not really,' he said. 'We'll have to make it up as we go along.'

*   *   *

We started with the floor, which was a foot deep in ancient manure. I said I wouldn't touch anything that came out of the back end of a cow and Coley said he couldn't make me and started shovelling on his own. But the stuff was so old there was no smell off it any more. It was just like black earth. I watched for a while to make sure, then picked up another shovel and joined in.

Before we had the first load in the transport box all the plasters I'd put on my fingers had come off. They were cheap ones from the Two Euro shop that my ma bought for Dennis because they had pictures of the Simpsons on them. Completely useless. But the shovel rubbed different parts of my hands from the bale strings so I was able to keep going, and in the end the new blisters I got that day caused me more problems than the old ones.

When the transport box was full we got in the tractor and took it over to old Mr Dooley's vegetable garden. He was delighted when he seen what we had for him.

'That's the best fertilizer in the world,' he said. 'I've had my eye on that stuff for ten years. I thought I'd be dead and buried before you got around to moving it.'

He walked ahead of the tractor and showed us where to dump it.

'That's it!' he shouted, when Coley tipped up the transport box and the black stuff came tumbling out. 'That's perfect. I'll have cabbages the size of beach balls next year with that stuff.'

'God help us all,' said Coley, when we were driving back to the sheds again. 'As if we didn't get enough cabbage as it is.'

There wasn't much in the way of a floor in those old sheds. The black stuff got grittier as we went down, that was all. When we came to the bottom of the dividing wall Coley said we'd gone far enough. We levelled off the floors and hosed the walls, then went in for a cup of tea.

Afterwards I thought we'd be making concrete for the floors but we were nowhere near that stage yet. We had to dig drains first, from the middle of both floors all the way across the grassy patch and down to the corner where it met the top meadow. It was back-breaking work with spades and picks and shovels. My new blisters were swelling up and bursting on my hands. Coley gave me better plasters but they wouldn't stay on neither. I kept changing my grip on the tools but whenever I did I just got a new blister in a new place.

'Don't you ever get them?' I said to Coley.

'I do,' he said. 'A few. In the spring. When I wake up from hibernation.'

I kept asking myself why I was doing this. No one was forcing me to do it. I could tell Coley to bullock off with his meanlings and do it himself. There was nothing in it for me. I didn't give a fuck about Swedish Lars or his ma or their Skoda or anything. At least ten times that day I decided I'd had enough and I was going home. I never talked myself out of it or changed my mind, but somehow I just didn't go.

It wasn't that I was mad about Coley or anything. He was funny sometimes and he was easy-going but he was nothing like the lads in Dublin. There was no edge to him. No danger. He was wet. He did what his da did, and his grandda. It wasn't because of him that I stayed. I think it was just because there was something happening. Even if it was only digging a drain or stacking bales or shovelling shit, it was still something happening. At home, nothing ever happened.

We were digging all morning, then after dinner we laid the pipes, which didn't hurt my hands or my shoulder, and then we filled in the channel again, which did. We were just finishing up when PJ came home early from work.

'Is that all you've got done?' he said.

I showed him my hands, and he said, 'Jesus, Mary and Joseph. We'll have to get you a set of chain mail or something.'

Then he reached into his pocket and sorted me out another tenner.

'I know what this is,' I said. 'It's blood money.'

He laughed, and said to Coley, 'Go up, the two of you, and count the cattle in the bog. And don't let him touch anything.'

There were about five bikes in the shed. Coley took out his own one, then pulled out two more before he found one with air in the tyres. He still had to pump it before I could use it. It was an old racer with thin tyres and drop handlebars. When we went past the house PJ came out again. He waved us down and we stopped.

'Is that Matty's bike?' he said to Coley.

'No,' said Coley. 'It's one Tom had.'

PJ turned to me. 'Give me back that tenner,' he said.

'No way,' I said. 'You gave it to me. It's mine.'

He reached out his hand. 'Give it back.'

I felt in my pocket. I still had the twenty from yesterday. I gave him back the tenner.

'Right,' he said. 'That bike is yours. You won't need any more lifts up, now.'

'Thanks, Mr Dooley,' I said.

'Just don't try and ride it to Dublin, that's all,' he said.

I stood up on the pedals and raced Coley along the road. My bike was old and the gears were a bit out of synch, but it was still a lot faster than his. I told him so when he called me back to turn in the bog road. I'd sailed straight past it.

'True for you,' he said. 'But you'll wish you had my suspension when we go down here.'

I did, and there were more jokes about bullocks, but I was happy as Larry with my bike. I'd had two bikes in Dublin – one my ma bought me from the second-hand shop and a newer one that I robbed. But some other fucker robbed them both off me. It's not worth having a bike in Dublin. There's no way you can keep them. They always get robbed.

Their bog field was miles wide and it took us ages to walk into all the corners and find all the cattle that were supposed to be there. There were only about thirty but they were split up into little groups and we couldn't go home until we seen them all and made sure none of them were sick or dead. I wouldn't know the difference anyway. Coley said: 'You'll learn.'

I said, 'Bullocks I will.'

It was only about four o'clock when we got back but PJ sent me home and told me to soak my hands in vinegar and leave them uncovered overnight and then to find some bandages or something for the morning.

I left my bike in the front hall because none of the sheds had locks on them and I was afraid someone would take it. My ma said: 'Where did that come from?'

'PJ gave it to me,' I said.

'That was nice of him,' she said. 'Did you ask him for the DVD cable?'

'No,' I said. 'Ask him yourself.'

There was loads of shopping on the kitchen table. A big bag of dog food, and loads of nice things that we didn't usually have. Orange juice and Crunchy Nut Cornflakes and a big tin of Roses and four packets of fags. My ma didn't say a thing when I put one of them in my pocket.

'I thought you had no money,' I said. 'I thought

you gave it all to the taxi driver. Where did you get all this?'

'The shop in the village,' she said. 'They let you put it on the slate and pay at the end of the week.'

34

That night the rattle of the dog flap woke me. I was out of bed before I was even awake, and running down the stairs. The kitchen was empty. I turned on the outside light and unlocked the back door and went out on to the concrete path.

The dog was out there. It was only the fucking dog, after all that. It turned its head to look at me and wagged its tail, and then looked back the way it was facing, towards the hedge. Something rustled at the bottom of it and I got a glimpse of an animal there before it went through and vanished from sight. A badger. I'd only seen pictures of them before. It was bigger than I thought it would be. Fat. I was glad I seen it.

'Are you coming in?' I said to the dog. It wagged its tail again but it stayed where it was.

'Stupid dog,' I said, and went in.

Just to be sure, I looked in on Dennis. He was fast asleep in his own bed, with Jimjam bunny in his arms.

35

The next day I was driving all day, following the silage contractors. They were cutting the big green meadows that lay across the road from the bog field. They had these amazing machines that cut the grass and wrapped it in big round bales with black plastic, like a sweet factory or something, only massive. My job was to pick up the bales they made and put them all in a corner of the field, where they could be collected any time they were needed. It was easy work, picking up the bales with this special front-loader, which was just two prongs, and driving backwards and forwards. Coley was working again and PJ was gone most of the time, too, so it was just me and the contractors, and they were going too hard and fast to stop and chat, except when they had a coffee break and brought out their flasks. That Kevin Talty fella, the one who owned the land across the road, came over one time. He asked them when they were coming to do his fields, and they told him it would be tomorrow or the next day. He asked them if it would cost the same as last year and they said it would, more or less, depending on the number of bales. Then he asked them who I was.

'He's the lad from Dooleys',' one of them said.

'He's not,' said Kevin Talty. 'I know all their lads. He's not one of them.'

I wouldn't mind, but I was standing right beside them. He just kept on talking like I wasn't there.

'Who is he?'

The contractors said it again, that I was from Dooleys', but Talty wouldn't listen to them, and he never once looked at me so I could tell him. I was looking at one of the lads and we were trying not to laugh.

'I don't know who he is,' Kevin Talty said, and he walked off across the field, talking to himself and shaking his head.

After that we started up again and moving those bales around got boring, so I had plenty of time to think, and mostly what I thought about was Dublin and the lads.

I couldn't make out how it had all gone pear-shaped so fast. I knew it was partly to do with Mick being in jail, but that wasn't the only thing. What was Fluke thinking of, shacking up with a girl with two kids? And Beetle was suddenly only interested in getting off his head. When he wasn't asleep, that was. Or had he always been like that? Putting up with the other stuff because he knew it brought in the money for the gear?

What we needed was a good race. That was the problem, I thought. We hadn't had a chance to get hold of any cars lately, because I was away all week and I just never came back at the right time. But we would do it again, some time soon, and then we would be back where we should be. Good friends, enjoying life together.

There was nothing like a race to get the blood up. People used call it joyriding, but you weren't supposed to call it that any more, in case kids like us got the idea that it was fun. Dickheads, whoever thought of that. As if a word could make any difference.

36

The next morning my ma was up before me again, making toast.

'Is there another funeral?' I asked her.

'No,' she said. 'I just felt like getting up early. Is there something wrong with that?'

'Are you going to Ennis?' I said.

'I might be,' she said.

'I need a bike lock. And a charger for my iPod.'

'Your what?'

'IPod. Have you never heard of an iPod?'

'Of course I have,' she said. 'I just didn't think you had one.'

'Well I have,' I said. 'But I haven't got a charger for it.'

'Where d'you get that, then?'

'Any electrical shop.'

'I meant where did you get the iPod?' she said.

'I found it in the street,' I said.

Coley and PJ had both gone to work that day but Grandda Dooley was out in the yard, waiting for me. It gave me the feeling that I was a nuisance pet that someone in the family had to mind, but Mr Dooley seemed happy enough with the job.

On the way across the yard he looked at my feet. My trainers were all mud from digging drains with Coley, and they were split in two places. I didn't care. They were old ones. I had better ones at home.

'We'll have to get you some Wellingtons,' said Mr Dooley. 'I'll lend you a pair of mine.'

'I'm all right in these,' I said.

'Suit yourself,' he said.

We hitched up the mower on the tractor again and he went into his tool shed and came out with a scythe with a long, curving handle. He looked like the Grim Reaper, coming across the yard. He let me drive and we went down into the rough meadows that lay between their farm and my house. At the bottom of the first one he made me stop and we got out.

'You need to cut all these rushes, here,' he said.

There were a lot of them, crowded in together, dark bluey green. There were clear patches of grass in between where the cattle had been grazing, but if I had to make a bet I would say the rushes were winning. Mr Dooley pointed to the higher slopes of the field.

'You can do those parts with the mower,' he said, 'but you can't take the tractor into these corners here. It'll get bogged. You'll have to use the scythe down in these bits. I'll show you how to do it.'

I followed him. My feet squelched in the boggy ground and brown water filled my trainers. Mr Dooley began to cut rushes with the scythe. He just used the tip of it, mainly, sliding it round in a circular motion just above the ground. The blade made a gorgeous, soft, crunchy sound and rushes dropped behind it like fallen soldiers.

'You have to keep the blade level with the ground,' he said. 'And just cut a small few at a time. There's no point in trying to use the whole of the blade. They're too thick.'

He showed me. The scythe thunked into the tight base of a big clump and stopped dead.

'Do you want to try?' he asked me.

'No,' I said. 'I'll get the hang of it on my own.' I didn't want to do it with him watching me. I hated people correcting me.

'All right,' he said. 'But be careful with it.'

'I know,' I said. 'You could shave yourself with that.'

He grinned and nodded. 'But the edge won't last all that long,' he said. 'I'll come down after a while and bring the stone and show you how to sharpen it.'

He walked off up the meadow. He was quite fit for an old fella but I noticed he stopped a couple of times like he was just taking a look around, but really it was so he could catch his breath.

Mowing the rushes was all right. They made a much better sound than the grass did when they died. You could hear the mower blades slice through them and the rattle when they fell over. And it was quick, cutting through one line and then swinging round and going back in to do the next, and then on to the next patch.

Some bits looked really great when I was finished them – all the cut rushes lying flat in the same direction, making a pattern on the ground.

I was careful, but I didn't hang around. I wanted to get the mowing done so I could have a go with the scythe. But I did stop for a while at one stage. It was over near the big hedge that ran between the field where I was and the one beside it, where the little hill was with the ring fort on it. I had to get right up against the hedge to cut one thick patch of rushes and that was when I seen the little path. It ran along beside the hedge for a while, then disappeared through it, and there was a small little tunnel through the hedge, really neat. I left the tractor running and walked over to have a better look. There were footprints on the path, all mashed up together in the mud. Badger, I was sure. This is where it came, after it went under the hedge outside our back door. Along here and through and away towards its hole under the fort. I heard myself telling Fluke and Beetle, showing them like one of those people on the wildlife programmes on TV. An expert on the countryside. No way they'd ever come down here, though. Not in a million years.

I went back to the tractor and finished the mowing, then left it on the hill and went down to where Mr Dooley had left the scythe, leaning up against a gate post. When I picked it up I remembered I was supposed to have soaked my hands in vinegar and wrapped them in bandages, but the day on the silage had given them a bit of time to recover and they didn't feel too bad. Anyway I didn't care. It was worth a bit of pain to have a go with that long blade.

But I couldn't make it work. I tried to swing it the way he showed me but every time I did the tip of it would get jammed in a clump of roots or dig into the ground. I tried again and again. I changed my grip, I concentrated on keeping the blade level, I tried out wider swings and shorter ones. Nothing worked. I got annoyed and swung it harder and faster. I jarred my shoulder and opened up my blisters all over again. Suddenly I was in a red rage, hacking at the green fuckers with the middle of the blade, still getting nowhere.

And then I stopped and looked at myself. What the fuck was I doing? I was standing out in the middle of a field, up to my ankles in bog water, hurting myself and sweating like a pig. Whose idea was this? It wasn't mine. This wasn't fun. This wasn't even something happening. This was pure slave labour. Child abuse, even.

I looked up at the two farmhouses at the top of the hill. The bungalow windows were dark, like two empty eyes looking down at me. What did Grandda Dooley do all day when he wasn't sharpening things? Was he watching me now?

I didn't care. I threw the scythe down in the rushes and walked home across the fields.

37

My ma wasn't in the house. There was a note left on the table.

GONE 2 DUBLIN 2 SIGN ON
BACK 2MORO FEED THE DOG

I stared at it. I thought she was supposed to be signing on in Ennis. How could she go to Dublin without telling me? How could she go without bringing me?

I threw the bag of dog food on the floor and the biscuits flew everywhere. I raged through the house, upstairs and down, not knowing where I was going or what I was looking for. The bitch, the cow, the slapper, the slag. She couldn't do that to me. I'd get her for this.

I stopped halfway down the stairs and rang her on the mobile. I didn't let her say anything. I just shouted a load of abuse at her and said: 'You can't do this to me! I'm coming up after you!' And then I hung up.

She didn't think I could. She didn't know about the blood money. I felt it in my pocket. My bus fare. All I had to do was get to Ennis.

I needed my bike. That made me stop and think. It was up in the yard, which meant I had to go back and get it. I didn't care. That old man couldn't stop me. I ran out of the house and jumped the wall and ran back across the first field and into the second.

Shite. He was coming down the hill with a pair of wellies in one hand and some kind of stone in the other. I didn't stop.

'Sorry, Mr Dooley,' I said. 'My ma's run off to Dublin. I have to go after her.'

I ran straight past him and up to the yard. I thought of taking Coley's bike because it was newer and smarter, but my own one was faster so I took it. I went down the road and straight past our house. On the way into the village I seen Mrs Grogan looking out her window and I gave her the finger. I stood on the pedals and the bike just flew. It was a brilliant bike, even if it was old.

The brakes weren't great, but I didn't have to use them very often. I thought about getting them fixed, but then I thought I'd never see the bike again because I had no lock for it and I would have to leave it behind me when I went for the bus. I didn't care. I pedalled till my legs felt like they were on fire but I didn't let it slow me down, and after another while they stopped hurting and I couldn't feel them at all.

When I got to the bus station I left the bike against the wall. I was a bit wobbly and I had to stamp my feet a few times and steady myself up before I could walk properly. I'd just missed the Limerick bus and there wasn't another one for more than an hour, but I bought my ticket anyway. One way. This time there was no way I was coming back. Not ever.

But even so I didn't see the point of leaving my bike there for some scumbag to rob. You never knew. It was a good bike. Some time I might come back for it. So I went towards the edge of town and found a place where the river crossed under the road and I followed a side street until I found a place where I could get down to the path. There were thick trees and bushes down there and I hid it in a big bramble bush. I hid it so well you couldn't see it at all, not even if you were walking along the river.

I smoked a fag going back up the road into town, and then I seen the supermarket and I knew what I wanted more than anything was a drink. So I went up there and took a couple of cans of lager and went to the checkout.

'ID?' said the woman behind the till.

'I left it at home,' I said. 'I'm nineteen.'

'Sorry,' she said. 'No ID, no sale. We're not allowed to.'

'That's ridiculous,' I said. 'I never get asked for it.'

'Sorry,' she said again, and put the two cans in under the counter.

I left her till and looked along the checkout desks. There was a woman further down who was going having a party. She was packing gallons of drink into those square green bags. She wouldn't miss a few cans of it.

I had the six-pack in my hand and was out through

the main doors before the security guard knew what was happening. On the way across the car park I thumped every car I passed and laughed, legging it down the road, hearing the howling of all those alarms. At the end of the road I looked back. The security guard was beat and he was talking on the phone. No problem. It'd be ages before the guards got there and I would be long gone, in under the bramble bush with my bike.

By the time I woke up I'd missed the bus to Limerick, and probably the next one as well. I felt like death warmed up. My guts were full of acid and my head was spinning, and on top of all that my legs were so stiff from the twenty-k cycle that I could hardly move them at all.

There were five empty cans under the bike. I didn't mean to drink that many. It was always the same with me, though. Once I got started drinking I couldn't stop. But I never used to go asleep when I was drinking with the lads. Beetle was the one who did that, not me. I always stayed awake, having the craic, looking for whatever came next.

I threw up into the bushes beside me but it didn't help. There wasn't much there, just a few dribbles. I looked at the time on my phone. It was half four and there would be plenty more buses, but I knew I couldn't go now. I felt too ill and I'd lost my nerve. Ennis was a small place and there was a good chance that someone would recognize me. In any case, I didn't feel angry with my ma now. I didn't feel anything except sick and cold and lonely. I wished I was dead.

There was nothing new in that. I often thought of hanging myself or getting hold of a gun and blowing out my brains. That would teach my ma. I knew fellas who had done it, too. Everyone said, 'Poor lad,' and 'What must he have been thinking of?' but I never felt sorry for them. I just thought, fair play to him. He had the guts to get out.

I sat and looked at the river until I was able to move again. Then I put the can that was left in the inside pocket of my jacket and dragged myself and my bike out of the brambles. Now the backs of my hands were all scratched, and between the backs and the fronts there was more red than white. I would have laughed if I hadn't felt so sick.

I got back up to the road and got on the bike and made my legs turn the pedals, even though they didn't want to. I went away from the town centre and tried to find my way through the back streets to my own road, but I didn't know the place at all and after ten minutes I was just getting more and more lost. It started to rain. I asked a girl with a babby in a pushchair and she gave me directions. I had to go back past the supermarket. I just dropped my head and pedalled past and didn't look up again until the place was way behind me.

It was lashing rain and I was soaked. Three times along the road I stopped and puked into the ditch, but whatever was making me sick didn't come out. Every time I stopped I thought of my bus ticket and wondered whether to go back, but I couldn't face the thought of seeing people. I'd rather be in the house on my own.

I should have eaten something before I left town. Every stretch I did on the bike was shorter than the one before. My legs were giving out. After about two kilometres I got off and pushed it. That's what I was doing when PJ and Coley passed me in the car and stopped to pick me up.

'I'm all right,' I said. 'I'll get home on my own.'

'You don't look all right to me,' PJ said. He was in a bad mood. He took the bike off me and put it in the hatchback with the front wheel hanging over the back seat. He couldn't close the door so he tied it to the tow bar with a piece of baler twine, I got in the back seat and watched the bike wheel turning beside me.

PJ started the car and drove off. He looked at me in the rear-view mirror. 'Have you been drinking?' he said.

'No,' I said. 'I think I've got the flu or something.'

He sighed. 'My father rang me,' he said. 'He told me you'd run off looking for your mother.'

I wished he would shut up. The exhaust fumes were coming in the open back door and making me sicker than ever.

'She went up to Dublin to sign on,' I said. 'She never told me she was going.'

'When is she coming back?'

'Tomorrow, she said.'

'Well it's not the end of the world,' he said. 'You can come up and stay with us tonight if you don't want to be on your own.'

I seen Coley turn quickly and look at him, but I couldn't read his face.

'No thanks,' I said. 'I'll be grand on my own.'

He went quiet for a bit, and then he said to Coley, 'How's the job going?'

Coley laughed. 'If you lined up all the cans I stacked today you'd end up in China.'

'Why didn't you, then?' I said, but I don't think he got it.

'Some lad stole a six-pack off a woman at the checkout,' he said. 'He set off all the car alarms in the car park.'

'I heard that,' said PJ. 'Everyone went out in the street, wondering what was going on.'

Oh, that was brilliant. The whole town of Ennis brought to a standstill. I smiled to myself in the back, but then I caught sight of PJ's eyes in the mirror, watching me. I straightened my face and closed my eyes and prayed I wouldn't puke my ring up in his car.

Afterwards I wished I'd stayed at Coley's. I wondered what the bedrooms looked like. Tidy as the kitchen, probably, with flowery covers on all the duvets, and pillow cases that matched. My ma had stuff like that in the hot press in Dublin but she never got round to putting them on the beds. She said they only got dirty and she couldn't spend her whole life washing them.

But by the time I wished I'd stayed it was too late. It was already dark and you'd have needed a crane to get me out of the house after what I found under the stairs.

38

The first thing I did when I got into the house was get out of my wet clothes, and then I took two Solpadine and went to bed. After an hour or two I got up and made myself some sausages and beans. The dog had eaten most of the biscuits on the floor and was lying under the table with a big bloated gut. I picked up the bag and what was left in it and put it on top of the fridge.

I made tea and decided to play on my Xbox. I was looking for something new to play but when I was going through the bag with the games in it I came across two DVDs that Mick gave me a few weeks back. They were copies of something and there was nothing written on them. All he said when he gave them to me was 'You'll enjoy them. Make sure your ma doesn't get her hands on them.'

I had no idea what they were, but knowing Mick they were probably hard porn or snuff movies or something. And I might not get a better chance to look at them for months. I was going back downstairs with them when I remembered about the cable for the DVD. I swore, and thought of biking up to Dooleys' to see if PJ had got one for it. But then I remembered what he said when he was taking my bike out of the back of his car.

'What's that mattress doing there?'

It was still draped over the turf barrow, even wetter now than it was when my ma first washed it.

'It got wet,' I told him. 'My ma's getting you a new one.'

He shook his head as if his team had just scored an own goal.

'She'd better,' he said. 'She'd better.' And he sounded like he meant it. He sounded like a man with a violent temper, just waiting to erupt.

So I didn't feel like going and asking him for anything. The time wasn't right. I tried to remember what my ma had said. There was somewhere in the house it might be. Where was it? Under the stairs, that was it. Except all the Swedish bloke's junk was piled in on top of it.

I didn't mind. My legs were still shaky but there was nothing wrong with my arms. I opened the door and began to haul the stuff out. There were bags of clothes at the top, jammed in so tight that some of them split when I pulled them out and shoes and boxer shorts spilled out. Underneath them there was two boxes, a plastic one and a wooden one with a lid. I opened the wooden one but there was only paints and brushes and chalks and stuff. Under that there was a computer and a printer and a big old heavy monitor, all of them practically antiques. And under that was a stack of banana boxes, all crammed full of books.

How could anybody have so many books? You

couldn't read that many books in twenty years. Maybe he was selling them or something. The second-hand bookshops in Dublin would give you a few euros for them, but books weren't worth robbing. Not unless they were really special ones.

One time Beetle set up an ebay account using his da's credit card and bank account details. Me and the others used go over there and search through millions of things on ebay, looking to see what made the most money. Fluke found a book on there that went for twelve hundred pounds. Pounds, not euros. And some musical instruments made a packet, old guitars and violins. And anything to do with boats and sailing. Mick copied pictures and pretended we were selling things. People sent him questions about them and we had to make up the answers. But we got caught before we got paid for anything and Mick's da went mental. I think he did something to Mick that time. I think Mick was worse after that.

I dragged out the banana boxes. One of them split and all the books fell out. I climbed in over them and hunted around for the DVD cable. There was that kind of junk in there all right, on three thin shelves at the back. A lamp with a hole burned in the shade. A box of those old plugs with round pins, absolutely no use to anybody any more. Under the bottom shelf was a load of tangled electrical wire and extension cords and stuff, but no DVD lead. I was just throwing them all back when I spotted the edge of something sticking out of a hole in the wall. It was a plastic bag. I got down on my knees and pulled it out. There was something in it, a book or something.

The whole of the kitchen floor was covered with stuff. I picked my way through it and sat down on a chair and opened the plastic bag. The book inside it was a kind of diary, but it didn't say diary on it or anything. It had a picture of a bird on the front, all different colours. It came open at a page that had something stuck in it with sellotape. A bunch of hairs. They were kind of black with grey in them, or grey with black in them. There was six or eight of them, stuck to the top of the page and dangling down. They were longer than mine but shorter than my ma's. Beside them there was a bubble with an arrow pointing to them, and inside the bubble there were words, but I couldn't read any of them except DOG FLAP.

I shifted around so the book was directly under the light. We always had it turned on in there because the window was too small to let in enough daylight. Under the bubble was a picture of the dog flap with a little bunch of hairs stuck in one corner, and under that was a kind of close-up of the dog flap with a little face looking in and its hair caught in the hinge. The face was all sharp – sharp nose and a sharp chin and sharp ears – and it was old and wrinkled. The eyes were just two empty black holes. I knew it was only a drawing but it scared the shite out of me.

I looked out the window. It was still light but it

wouldn't be for long. I looked at the dog flap hanging on its hinges. I thought about Dennis and his night-time games. I wished my ma was home.

I looked back at the book. There were more words around the cartoon drawings and when I tried to make them out I realized why I couldn't. They weren't in English at all, but some other language. Must have been Swedish. I turned over the page. There was only writing on it and I turned again. There was another drawing, of a badger disappearing through the hedge, just like I'd seen it. In his drawing it had a big fat behind and its back legs were scrabbling and throwing up stones. He was good at drawing.

On the next page was another badger, and a rabbit sitting up on its heels, and a black bird. Underneath and in between was more writing, and I was about to turn over again when I seen a few lines written in English. They said:

It is well established in all the folk tales that the fairies had the ability to change their shape. Ravens, hares and badgers appear to be the most common forms.

There was more in Swedish, and then another bit in English.

The Tuatha de Danaan were defeated and banished to live beneath the ground.

I turned over. There was another picture, of a wooden door in the side of a hill, and lines coming out of it like it was shining. And more in English.

The fairy folk were known as the 'sidhe', which

means, literally, a hill. Hence the hill people, or the people who lived under the hill.

There were more bits in English like that on other pages, but I kept turning and looking for more pictures. There was one of the fairy fort where Coley took me, the one behind our house with the hole in it. And a couple of pages further on there was another one of a badger, and then the dog flap again, with the little green bowl in front of it, coloured in.

I shut the book and pushed it away. The man was a head-banger. As bad as Dennis. You couldn't have people who turned into badgers. Then I had a sudden idea and opened the diary again, to the page with the hairs on it. Maybe that was the mix-up. Maybe it was just a badger that came in through the dog flap at night, looking for milk.

I looked closely at the little bunch of hairs. Could they have come off a badger? I didn't know what badger hair looked like. These were certainly the right kind of colour. But when I fingered them I wasn't sure. They were fine and silky, like Dennis's. They had the feel of human hair to me.

39

I wrapped the diary up in its bag again and shoved it back into the hole in the wall. Then I pushed the banana boxes back in, and stuck the broken one on top of the others and began to pick up the books that had fallen out of it. *Irish Myths and Legends. Gods and Fighting Men. Fairy Tales. Animal Stories.* They all had those little coloured page-markers that the girls use in school. I opened one at a marked page and there was a paragraph gone over with a green highlighter but I didn't read it. I'd already seen too much.

I jammed everything back under the stairs and wedged the door shut with Dennis's Bart Simpson toothbrush. It was beginning to get dark. The window was blue, like there was water behind it. I locked the back door and looked at the dog flap. I wanted to shove something up against it, but what would I do with the dog, then? I thought of leaving it outside but I didn't know what would happen if I did. It might die or something.

I went in and turned on the TV, but I couldn't follow anything. I was too busy listening for noises at the back door. I wished I'd got on the bus. I could be in Dublin now, instead of sitting here like an eejit, scared out of my wits.

I'd had enough of this place with its fairies and

badgers and tractors and big, hefty country men. I wanted to go home. I wanted to get Fluke and Beetle back into shape and working with me again. And if they weren't into doing that any more I'd just have to find some other lads who were. I knew loads of fellas in the flats. I just never bothered hanging round with them. I never needed to. But it wouldn't be hard to find lads and show them where the action was. I knew how to get keys for cars, and I knew how to drive them and where to go. I knew where that house was in Coolock and I had the password.

But I needed somewhere to live up there, that was the problem. I remembered the strange woman who had opened my ma's door. That was scary. I needed my own place. But that would cost money.

Something cracked somewhere in the house. I held my breath and crept to the kitchen door, listened for a minute, then opened it. The dog wagged its tail. I let out my breath. I couldn't go on like this all night. I wouldn't be able to sleep a wink.

That was when the idea came to me. I felt like a right eejit, but I did it anyway. I took out the little green bowl and filled it with milk, unlocked the back door and left it out on the window ledge. I was half laughing at myself, but it made me feel better. And then I had another thought. I had an old tobacco tin upstairs where I kept my stash when I had one. I ran up and got it and emptied the skins and bits of cardboard out of it, then brought it down and put three of the Roses inside it. I left it out beside the green bowl on the window ledge. It was a little test for my friend, the badger. It might be able to stand up and drink milk out of a bowl, but there was no way an animal would get the lid off that tin.

Fuddy bear woke me once during the night and the hairs stood up on the back of my neck when I went across the kitchen floor. But the rest of the night I slept like a log. If the dog went out I never heard it. And when I woke, early in the morning, I found I had a new plan fully formed in my head.

I wouldn't go to Dublin that weekend. There was no point when I only had a fiver and nowhere to go. I would keep my bus ticket and wait until I had some more cash. I would work for PJ and if I was lucky he might give me a tenner a day. Maybe not every day. Maybe thirty a week. And my ma would give me another twenty, and maybe I could squeeze her for a bit more. If I gave up the fags, or just smoked hers, I could save what I had until I got enough to get myself a room somewhere. I could do that. I knew I could. And once I was in Dublin I'd survive. If I didn't have to share what I robbed with Fluke and the others I could live like a king.

I ran down and into the shower, then I dressed myself in clean clothes from head to foot. In my room I had a pair of designer hiking boots that I took off a lad who strayed too far out of his own part of town. I'd been saving them for best, but I put them on now. It was time to make a good impression, and they were Gore-Tex, so they would keep my feet dry and all.

I bolted down my breakfast and burned my mouth with the tea. I was in such a rush to get to work early that I almost forgot about the green bowl and the tin, but I remembered when I was going out the gate and I dropped the bike to go and look.

The milk was gone but the tin was still where I left it, up against the corner of the window frame. I knew I was right and I reached out and picked up the tin to prove it to myself. But the tin was as light as air, and nothing rattled inside it.

I looked in to make sure. Someone or something had opened it, taken out the chocolates and put it carefully back again.

It wasn't a badger that done that.

40

PJ was having his breakfast when I landed up at the house. When he opened the door he had egg yolk on the side of his mouth, but I didn't laugh.

'I didn't expect to see you today,' he said.

'Why not?' I said.

'You said you had the flu.'

'It's gone,' I said. 'It can't have been the flu after all.'

He looked me up and down and seen the clean clothes.

'You'd better come in,' he said.

I followed him into the kitchen and sat on the chair beside the range.

'Coley and myself are both working again today,' he said. 'And my father isn't happy about the way you left his scythe yesterday.'

'I meant to pick it up,' I said.

'He's very particular about his tools.'

'I just forgot,' I said. 'What with my ma going off like that and all.'

He didn't say anything, so I said, 'I won't do it again.'

He shook his head and sighed, and he said to Coley, 'Give him a cup of tea.'

Coley got up for a clean mug and poured me one.

The tea in their house was different from ours. It had leaves in the bottom. It tasted thicker. Better.

'There isn't really anything for you to do,' PJ said. 'Not that you can do on your own.'

'I'll do Coley's sheds,' I said. 'I'll put the new floors down.'

'Do you know how to lay concrete?' he said.

'No,' I said. 'But I can make it up as I go along.'

Coley laughed.

PJ drank his tea. The egg yolk was still on his face. I still didn't laugh. Coley got up and started clearing the table.

'We better go,' he said to his da.

'Shut up, Coley,' PJ said. Then he looked at me.

'There is a job you can do,' he said. 'If you promise not to set the whole county on fire.'

This time he put a special yoke on the back of the car for my bike. He brought me to the tool shed and handed me out a bush saw and a pair of thick green welders' gloves and a little hatchet. Then he went back in the house and got a big pile of newspapers.

'You've your own cigarette lighter, haven't you?' he said.

I said I had. He drove me to a big steep field about three kilometres the other side of the village. He said he bought it a few years ago and it was cheap because it was so badly neglected. Last summer himself and Coley cut down all the gorse with the chainsaw and now it needed to be gathered up and burned.

When we got there he showed me where to light the fire, well in from the road and the hedge. He said I could light another one on the other side of the hill as well, to save me dragging the bushes all the way over.

'Don't burn it all in one go,' he said. 'Keep the fire ticking over and put on the bushes as you gather them.'

'I will,' I said. 'I won't go mad.'

'There's a few green bushes we missed,' he said. 'You can cut them yourself. If you put them on with the dry stuff they'll burn all right. And don't go home and leave it blazing. Let it die well back before you leave it.'

He left me with the bike and the tools and the newspapers and got back in the car. He still had egg on his face. As soon as they were gone I burst myself laughing.

The field was massive and the hill was steep, but there were worse ways of spending a day. It rained a bit but never enough to put my fires out, and the work kept me warm. The boots were brilliant as well. They kept my feet dry and they had soles like tractor tyres so they kept me from slipping down the steep bits of the hill. If I'd been wearing my trainers I would have spent most of the day on my arse.

I burned all the big bits first and it took me all morning, dragging the dead stuff and cutting the ones they'd missed. The fires were great. Every time I threw on a bush a big burst of sparks flew up in the sky. It was nearly a shame to be doing it in the day. Those fires would have looked deadly at night.

At dinner time I hid the tools under the far hedge and cycled home. I put on frozen chips but the oven was too slow and in the end I had bread and sausages and eggs.

I thought I was nearly finished the job but when I got back I could see all the small bits I'd left and I didn't like the way the field looked, so I started all over again. I found some old bale strings draped over the hedge beside the gate and tied some together so I could loop it through the small branches and drag a whole big bundle of them behind me. I got the little hatchet and cut down the small new bushes that were growing and I kept my fires ticking over and burned the lot. I should have been finished then and I was ready for a break and a cup of tea, but I still wasn't happy with the way the field looked. So I took the saw and the hatchet and cut all the stumps they had left behind right down to the ground, and I piled the bits beside the gate because most of them were good enough to burn on the fire at home and it was a shame to waste them. And when I'd done that I had one last go around the field, picking up any last bits I'd left and a few bits of old rubbish as well – fertilizer bags and silage plastic that had blown in there on the wind. They burned with a filthy black smoke and I had to keep moving around the fire to get away from the stink.

But I was happy with it at last, and I was just standing there admiring the clean field when PJ pulled up in the car. He came and stood beside me and looked at the field. He looked at it a lot longer than he needed to, and I was beginning to wonder if he'd seen something I'd missed. But he said: 'If you could sort yourself out you could build yourself a decent future.'

'Doing what?' I said.

'Anything you put your mind to, I'd say.' He looked at me. 'What would you like to do?'

I never knew anyone who worked – did a job, like. Except for Mick's da, and he was a head-banger. And Carmel, I suppose, although she did hairdressing and I wasn't about to do that.

'I don't know,' I said. 'Nothing.'

'Maybe you'll find something,' he said. 'You're young, yet. There's still time enough.'

Then he picked up the tools and the gloves and the newspapers that were left.

'You can get yourself home, can you?' he said.

I said I could, and he walked towards the car.

'Oi,' I called after him. 'Don't I get a tenner?'

He stopped and turned back, shaking his head and laughing at the same time.

'You're something else,' he said. But he gave me a tenner and I stood on the pedals of my bike all the way home.

41

My ma was just in the door. My good mood left me the minute I seen her. You couldn't move in the kitchen for plastic bags. Every one of those cost her fifteen cents out of her dole. We'd only been in the house for two weeks and she already had ten million of them stuffed in under the sink. It was the same in the flat in Dublin. Fluke used to say if my ma ever bought a proper shopping bag we could all go and live in Ballsbridge.

I pushed past her, dragging my bike through her shopping because I couldn't be bothered to go through and open the front door for it. She came after me.

'I got your bike lock,' she said. 'And your charger for the iPod.'

I came back. She started looking in the bags. Dennis was sitting on the floor, trying to make the dog eat an onion.

'I got you a T-shirt as well,' she said, pulling it out and handing it to me. 'In Moore Street.'

I couldn't believe it. She still thought I was into Lara Croft. I chucked it behind me on to the stairs. The bike lock was useless as well. It was one of those ones with a code number. You could cut through the wire on it with a scissors.

'Where did you get the money for all this stuff?' I said.

'It's Friday,' she said. 'I got my dole yesterday.'

'You must have spent it all, then,' I said.

'I did,' she said. 'And this cost a small fortune.'

She threw the iPod charger across at me. I looked at it and threw it back at her.

'That's the wrong kind, you stupid cow.'

'How can it be the wrong kind?' she said.

'It's the one that goes into a computer,' I shouted at her. 'In case you haven't noticed, we haven't got a fucking computer. How am I supposed to use that?'

'Well I didn't know,' she said. 'I went miles to find the right shop, and then it was the only one they had.'

I ran upstairs and threw myself on the bed. She always ruined everything. How could any mother be so totally, totally useless? And what were we supposed to live on now for the rest of the week? She could run up more of a bill at the shop for food and stuff, but what about my twenty euro?

I heard her mobile ring downstairs but she didn't answer it. Then mine rang. It was her sister, Carmel.

'What do you want?' I said.

'I want your ma. Is she there?'

'Why don't you ring her if you want her?' I said.

'She won't answer, that's why. Put her on, will you?'

'What do you want her for?'

'Just put her on, you little bollix!' She sounded really upset.

'What's it about?' I said.

'It's about money,' she said. 'When is it ever about

anything else? I had another money-lender banging my door down ten minutes ago. That's a hundred and seventy she owes me now and I can't afford it. I can't fight her fucking battles for her!' It sounded like she was crying. 'Do you know what those bastards are like?'

'Didn't she give you anything yesterday?' I said.

'How could she give me anything yesterday?' she said.

There was a nasty silence, while I realized my ma hadn't stayed with her last night. She must have stayed with Maura or someone. She never even told her own sister she was going up.

'Was she in Dublin yesterday?' Carmel said. I could hear she was beginning to go hysterical.

'Hang on,' I said.

I went down and handed the phone to my ma.

'Who is it?' she said.

'It's Carmel.'

She shook her head and pushed the phone back at me.

'Take it,' I said.

She went into the toilet and locked the door. I put the phone to my ear. Carmel was screaming abuse down the line. I hung up.

My ma was upset. She didn't talk to me while we had tea. She kept telling Dennis to stop singing and stop kicking the table and stop spilling the salt and messing with the sugar. Afterwards he wanted to feed Roses to the dog. She took the tin away from him and picked four of them out.

'If you're a very good boy you can take these to bed with you,' she said.

Then she put the tin up on the high shelf above the fitted cupboards where he couldn't reach it.

He went to bed early with his Roses. After he'd eaten them he wanted to come back down again but my ma wouldn't let him. While we watched the TV we could hear him up above our heads, shouting at Jimjam bunny and telling him he was bold. My ma thought it was funny, but it didn't put her in a good mood.

'I don't know how the money-lenders found Carmel,' she said to me. 'How could they? I never gave them her address or nothing.'

'Don't be stupid, Ma,' I said. 'Those fellas know everyone and everything. And if they don't, they have ways of finding out. They'll probably come after you down here even if Carmel doesn't tell them where you are.'

'Oh, don't say that, Bobby,' she said. 'I couldn't stand it. I'd top myself if they started coming down here after me.'

'You should have just stayed there and paid them,' I said. 'You should save some money instead of going mad every Friday.'

'Yeah, right,' she said. 'And you there with your hand out every second day. When it isn't in my purse.'

She stared at the TV, but she wasn't seeing it.

'I'm sick of having no money,' she said. 'I might get a job if I can find someone to mind his lordship.'

'Don't look at me,' I said.

'I wasn't,' she said. 'I wonder if Margaret Dooley would do it.'

'I can just see that,' I said, thinking of Margaret chasing around after Dennis in her spotless kitchen.

'She can't have much else to do,' my ma said, 'now that her own are all grown up. Maybe she would like to have him.'

'Ask her then,' I said.

'I might,' she said. 'But I'll have to find a job, first.'

As I went up to bed I thought about putting milk outside the window again, but I didn't want my ma to see me doing it. Coley's grandma told her to do it, after all, not me. It was her lookout if the place got filled with spooks and goblins. But when I was going off to sleep I kept thinking about my tobacco tin and wishing I hadn't left it out there. The bowl was still out there too, and both of them were empty.

I woke to the sound of an almighty crash. I ran down the stairs, but this time my ma was there before me, blocking the kitchen door. I looked in over her shoulder. There was a chair knocked over and Dennis was standing beside it, rubbing his knee. The tin was on the floor with a big dent in the side, and the Roses were scattered all over the place, sparkling like Christmas on Grafton Street.

Dennis was terrified. My ma flew across the room at him and he was screaming: 'It wasn't for me! It wasn't for me!'

I turned away. I didn't want to see what was coming. But I couldn't help hearing it, and I couldn't help feeling sorry for the poor little bollix. It wasn't his fault, after all. It wasn't him who gave her a taste for the Roses.

42

The dog ate most of the Roses in the night and then puked. Its puke was all full of bits of silver paper. My ma cleaned it up and put the ones that were left in the bin.

'He'll have to go,' she said. 'We can't keep him when he does things like that.'

'Yeah,' I said. 'You should send him to live with his da.'

'I meant the dog,' she said, but she laughed.

I didn't. 'I think we should get out of this house,' I said.

'What's wrong with this house?' my ma said. 'I thought you liked it.'

'Why did you think that?' I said. 'I never wanted to live down here in Culchieville. I want to go back home to the lads.'

'Well we're not going back,' she said. 'We're starting a new life and it's working out great.'

'It's not working out great,' I said. 'There's all this fucking mad stuff going on in the middle of the night. This place is haunted or something.'

'Don't you dare say things like that to me!' she said. 'You know how scared I get.'

'Well you should be scared,' I said. 'I'm fucking scared myself!'

She reared up and stood over me. 'It's that little bastard in there,' she said. 'But he won't get up in the night again if he knows what's good for him.'

He probably wouldn't either, after the belting she gave him last night. He'd probably wet the bed and get it in the neck for that instead.

'It's not just Dennis,' I said. 'Can't you get that into your thick head?'

She put her hands over her ears and sang '*Girls just want to have fun*' at the top of her lungs.

After my dinner I biked up the road to Dooleys'. I wasn't looking for work and I certainly didn't expect to knock any craic out of Holy Coley. But there was nothing to do and there was nowhere else to go. I was bored out of my brains at home.

Coley wasn't there anyway, and nor was PJ. But Margaret said: 'Matty's here, though. Why don't you go and see what he's doing?'

He was working on the Land Rover again. 'You must be Bobby,' he said when I went into the lean-to.

'And you must be the grease monkey.'

'That's me,' he said, holding out a hand. I shook it and came away with sump oil rubbed into my blisters. I looked under the bonnet of the Land Rover. There was still a lot of loose bits in there.

'I'm all ready to fit the new gasket,' he said. 'You came along at exactly the right moment. Want to give me a hand?'

'I don't mind,' I said. 'What do you want me to do?'

'I just need a bit of muscle,' he said. 'Coley is supposed to be helping me but he's got that old supermarket job. I think he only does it to get out of the farm work.'

'Doesn't he like farming then?' I said.

'Coley?' Matty said. 'Sure Coley's the brainbox out of all of us. He'll be a solicitor, that lad, you'll see. Loads of money and no fun. Wouldn't suit me at all.'

'Me neither,' I said.

He leaned into the engine again. 'There's the valves,' he said. 'All cleaned up and two new springs fitted. Now we just have to get the head back on. I had the gasket there a minute ago.'

He found a flat packet on the wing and peeled something out of it, and laid it over the top of the engine block. It was brilliant the way it fitted exactly over the lines.

'What does it do?' I asked him.

'Seals the whole thing,' he said. 'Keeps the air out and the power in. Very important little piece of kit, that is.'

'What's it called again?' I said.

'Head gasket,' he said. 'Have you got steady hands?'

I held them out to him. 'Steady as a rock.'

The cylinder head was sitting on the wing. Matty checked it over and brushed the bits of dust off it, then he took one side and I took the other. It was heavier than it looked.

'We have to line it up exactly,' he said. 'We don't want to disturb the gasket after all that.'

My arms were trembling with the weight of it but I didn't let it drop. I made sure it was lined up perfectly at my end and we both set it down at exactly the same moment. He came over to my side to check.

'Lovely job,' he said. 'Now . . .'

He picked up one of those square ice-cream tubs and took some bolts out of it and handed them to me, one by one. Then he poked around some more and took out some washers.

'How is it that you never get the same number out as you put in?' he said. 'It happens every time.'

He found one more, but that was all.

'You can put those ones in while I go hunt out some more washers,' he said.

He picked up a socket wrench and fiddled with something on the side of the handle. Then he gave it to me. I dropped one of the bolts into its hole in the cylinder head.

'Washer first,' Matty said.

'I know,' I said. 'I just forgot.'

The wrench only worked in one direction, then purred when you turned it back. I kept tightening and I could feel the bolt biting home, and then suddenly the wrench clicked and stopped working.

'Shite!' I said.

'What's up?' he said. He was raking through stuff in another ice-cream box.

'The wrench broke,' I said. 'I never done nothing to it. It just went.'

He came over and looked at it.

'Looks all right to me,' he said. 'Do another one till we see.'

I forgot the washer again but this time he said nothing and I remembered it myself, just in time.

'It's working again now,' I said. But then it clicked again, like something snapped inside it.

'There,' I said. 'See?'

He laughed at me. 'It's a torque wrench,' he said. 'It's supposed to do that. Here . . .'

He took it off me and showed me the handle. 'You can set it, see? Nearly every nut and bolt in a car engine has a torque setting. They're all written down in the manuals. You don't need them after a while, though. You get the general idea of what needs what.'

I looked at the torque wrench. I was in a hurry to use it again, now I knew what it was doing. Matty found two more washers in an old biscuit tin and came back, but he never took the wrench off me. He let me put all the bolts in for him.

'Will it go now?' I asked him.

He laughed. 'It'll be a while yet,' he said. 'There's another bit to do putting in the push rods and stuff. Then the rocker cover goes on, and that's the engine sorted. But after that I'll have to get a new carburettor for her, and a fuel pump.'

He kicked the Land Rover on one wheel, but not

very hard. 'She needs everything, really, the poor old creature. But that's the great thing about Land Rovers. There's nothing on them you can't fix if you have a mind to. And she'll be worth it in the end.'

He wiped his hands on a greasy rag then closed the bonnet.

'Do you know anything about bikes?' I said.

'Sure, bikes are easy,' he said. 'What needs doing?'

'It's all right,' I said. 'Just the brakes don't really stop it.'

He stood over my bike and looked at it. 'That was Tom's one,' he said. 'It was a great bike in its day.'

'It's a great bike now,' I said. 'It's faster than Coley's one.'

He bent and looked at the brakes. 'You need new blocks,' he said. 'But we might be able to squeeze a bit more out of these ones in the meantime.'

He straightened up again and looked at me.

'Are you busy today?'

'No,' I said, and my heart kind of leaped at the thought that there might be something cool to do with Matty. 'I've nothing to do at all.'

'I'll tell you what,' he said. 'I'll help you with your bike if you give me a hand afterwards.'

'Doing what?'

'Clearing up the workshop,' he said. 'It looks more like a breaker's yard every day.'

'Yeah,' I said. 'I'll do that, no bother. If you help me with the bike.'

The brakes only took a few minutes. It looked dead easy. The blocks on the front weren't too bad and Matty got them working really well.

'But don't go over the handlebars,' he said. 'Get the back ones changed.' He showed me how to do it myself and he let me keep the little spanner that fitted the nuts. I put it in my zip pocket. Then he set about adjusting the gears and he got it so all ten of them worked, and he showed me how to oil the chain. Then he turned on his electric air pump and put air into the tyres until they were hard as iron.

'Those old tubes won't last for ever, though,' he said. 'You'd better get a spare one when you get your brake blocks.'

'How much will that cost?' I said.

'Not much,' he said. 'Bike parts are cheap.'

43

When we went in for our tea my ma and Dennis were sitting in the kitchen. I couldn't believe it. It felt like an enemy invasion.

'What are you doing here?' I said to her.

'I was just out for a walk, weren't we, Dennis?' she said. 'We said we'd just call in.'

Margaret was making tea and ham sandwiches. Me and Matty washed our hands in the sink, but when he ate his sandwiches he still left big black pawprints on them. I wondered how much grease he had eaten and how much more he would eat before he died. I wondered if Coley was right, and he really was a greasoholic.

My ma and Margaret talked about the weather like it was headline news. Then Margaret asked my ma about her family in Dublin and she told her about how her ma had been killed a couple of years ago by stepping off the footpath in front of a lorry, and about how her da and his brother went to England and never came back. She never said about the hundred pounds he sent every Christmas, inside a card, in dirty old notes. That's only a hundred and fifty euro in the whole year, and my ma with the two of us to feed.

I looked at Matty. He was in the chair by the range, reading the newspaper. He had the right idea.

Then Margaret started on her family and what all her kids were doing. The one who was in Australia and the one who was in the hotel business – that was Tom – and the one who was married and had two children, one of them the same age as Dennis.

'So you're a grandma?' said my ma. 'You don't look old enough!'

She did, though. She looked ancient to me.

'You know what?' she said to my ma. 'While you're here I'll show you the photos of your house.'

She went off into the sitting room. I looked at Matty. I was hoping it was time for us to go back out again, but he just grinned and winked and went back to his newspaper.

Margaret came back with an album.

'Coley put them all in the one book for me,' she said. 'I thought that was a very clever idea.'

'It was,' said my ma. 'I've loads of photos some-where. I must get one of them books.'

Margaret opened the album. 'That one's from the old days,' she said. 'A very long time ago. The nineteen-thirties, maybe.'

My ma took Dennis on her lap so he could see, too. He was on his best behaviour after last night. I was look-ing at the pictures upside down but I could still see. The house was smaller, then. Just one storey, and the porch extension wasn't on it.

'The place was very tidy back in those days,' said Margaret. 'There was a little orchard there beside it, see? I wasn't here in those days. I never saw it.'

She turned over the page. There were more black-and-white photos. 'And that's Peggy, just after she married Joe and moved in.'

'Ah,' my ma said. 'Isn't she gorgeous?'

'And that's another one of her,' Margaret said. 'That was before her daughter was born. And that's Joe again, and the fella with him is PJ's father.

She turned over again and suddenly the house was in colour, and there was an old man standing outside the front door, smiling at the camera.

'Who's that?' my ma said.

'That's Joe again,' Margaret said. 'He was old by then. That was about ten years ago, I'd say.'

'But where's the daughter?' my ma said. 'Is there no pictures of her?'

'No,' Margaret said. She turned the page again. 'The house got very run down when he was old.'

It did, too. All the whitewash was gone off the walls and even upside down I could see that the roof was falling in and there were bits of plastic covering the holes and sandbags on ropes holding them on.

'He couldn't really manage it by himself,' Margaret said. 'By rights he should have gone into a home, but he wouldn't go, and we couldn't make him. We used do what we could for him. One or other of us would go down there every morning and evening, do his shopping and that. In the end I used send him a bit of dinner, with one of the lads.'

She turned over again. The roof was completely off the house.

'That was after we bought it,' she said. 'He didn't leave any will so the state took it over and a couple of years later they put it up for auction. We only wanted the land but the house came with it so we said we'd do it up. We thought one of the lads might like to use it but they never did yet.'

There was a few pages then of restoration photos. The walls being raised. The new roof timbers going in.

'There's Tom,' Margaret said. 'And that's Coley, holding the ladder.'

In the middle of these pictures my ma said, 'Why didn't he make a will? Why didn't he leave it to his daughter?'

'She died, God bless her,' Margaret said.

'Oh no,' said my ma. 'What of?'

''Tisn't certain,' Margaret said. 'She was never in good health. She was very small when she was born. She must have been very premature or something, and she never thrived.'

'They murdered her,' I said, and Matty put down his paper and looked at me. Both women looked at me as well. Dennis was bored with the photos and he was leaning back against my ma's shoulder, picking his nose.

'They were put away for it,' I said.

I know my ma thought I was lying but Margaret said: 'Nothing was ever proved. I don't believe they did it. Joe wouldn't hurt a fly, God rest him.'

'But she was mental,' I said. 'She thought the babby was a fairy. She died in prison.'

Margaret looked at me. 'You wouldn't want to believe everything Colman tells you,' she said.

'It wasn't Coley,' I said. 'It was his grandma told me. Isn't it true, then?'

Margaret didn't answer that. She turned over the next page, quickly, like she was trying to escape from something.

'There's the slates going on,' she said. 'We used the old ones again, and a few more we found around the place. Blue Bangors, they're called. New ones would never have looked right at all.'

But I could see my ma wasn't listening. She was still back a few pages, shocked by the story of the murder. I wished I'd said it to her before. We might have been back in Dublin by now if I had.

'And that's how it is now,' Margaret said. 'All finished. And there's Lars.'

He was standing beside the Skoda. I bent my head sideways to get a better look. Dennis sat up on my ma's lap, suddenly interested, and pointed at Lars.

'Stupid man,' he said. 'Why is he wearing a dress?'

'He's not wearing a dress,' my ma said. 'What are you on about?'

Dennis put his finger on Lars's blue lumberjack shirt.

'That's not a dress,' my ma said. 'It's a shirt, silly billy.'

I never heard her say 'silly billy' before. That was for Margaret's benefit.

'It's not a shirt,' Dennis said. 'It's a dress. It's the little woman's dress.'

My ma stood up and put him on her hip.

'Thanks for showing us the pictures,' she said to Margaret.

'You're welcome,' Margaret said. I could tell she was uncomfortable. The little session hadn't gone the way she expected. 'We must get one of you sometime. The three of you beside the house. I'll send Coley down some day with the camera.'

'Oh, yeah,' my ma said. 'That'd be nice.' But she wasn't happy. She was freaked out about living in a house where a child had been murdered.

'Come on, Bobby,' she said to me.

'I'm not going,' I said. 'I'm helping Matty clean up his workshop. I promised him.'

She didn't like it but there was nothing she could say in front of Margaret. So she went off with Dennis, and Margaret went off to put away the album and she didn't come back while Matty and me were still in the kitchen.

44

We worked right up until nine o'clock that evening. I never felt the time passing. The place was like a knacker's yard, with bits of old cars and tractors piled up against the walls and in the corners. We went through it all, sorting out what could be used again and what was useless. We put the good bits on steel racks Matty had in a locked shed at the side near the house, and the useless bits in blue chemical drums in the corner. He said the travellers came round looking for scrap metal and his da always liked to keep stuff like that for them. He said the same family had been coming round there for a hundred and fifty years.

Some of the bits were so heavy it took both of us to lift them. Matty told me what everything was while we worked our way through it all. There were cam shafts and con rods and CV joints and brake drums and clutch plates and differentials and gearboxes. He knew what car every part came from and he could tell by looking at it whether it was worth keeping or not. I did loads of unscrewing nuts and bolts and stuff, but he wouldn't let me use the torque wrench because he said you only needed that for tightening things up and not loosening them, and it was a top-of-the-range one and it cost him an arm and a leg. We kept all the nuts and bolts and washers and split pins we took off the useless stuff, but some of them were rusted on so tight I couldn't move them and Matty said to leave them.

When we had all the big stuff sorted out Matty went into the house and his ma gave him a rake of jam jars and biscuit tins and ice-cream cartons. Then we went through the pile of small things and put them all in their own special containers. There were ones for small and middle-sized nuts and small and middle-sized bolts and a jar for split pins and one for counter-sink screws, and a biscuit tin for all the electrical bits like fuses and wires, and a big jar for all the different kinds of washers. Then he emptied out all his old tins and jars and we sorted through all that as well, and he threw a lot of it out. And when we were done with that we picked up all the rags and swept the floor, and another load of small bits turned up in the sweepings and we went through those as well.

Matty never stopped talking but I didn't mind. I liked hearing about engines and driveshafts and synchromesh and everything, even if I didn't know what half of it was. He told me which cars were good and which were useless, and where they were all made, and which makes were getting better and which ones were getting worse, and what he would buy when he changed his car next year. I told him which cars I liked best to drive, but I know he didn't believe me and I didn't bother pushing it, even though he must have known about the Skoda.

The place looked brand new when we'd finished tidying up, but I didn't want to go. I kept looking around for something else that needed doing. When he offered me a twenty-euro note I said I didn't want it, and then I couldn't believe I'd said that.

He said, 'Go on, take it,' so I did, and that meant I had thirty-five euro towards the deposit on my room. But I still didn't want to go. I said: 'Will you be working on the cars again tomorrow?'

He said, 'I will, but I'll tip away on my own. My parents like a quiet Sunday.'

I still didn't go, and while I was hanging around with my hands in my pockets he said something that knocked me so far sideways I nearly went through the wall.

'How old is your mother? She looks very young. She doesn't look old enough to have a lad your age.'

I didn't answer him. It was like the sky suddenly changed colour, and nothing would ever be the same again.

45

I walked down the hill.

Fourteen. My ma was fourteen when she had me. It was no secret, I'd known it for years. But I was younger then, and fourteen was no different to me than eighteen or twenty-one. But not now, it wasn't. I was fourteen myself, now.

Fourteen. I couldn't get it out of my head. I would have loafed anyone who called me a kid. I thought of myself as a man, and so did the lads. But that didn't mean I was grown up. I couldn't imagine having my own kid and having to look after it and all.

'Bobby!'

I turned round. Matty was coming down the hill after me, pushing my bike. I waited for him.

'Are you all right?' he said.

'Grand,' I said. 'Why wouldn't I be?'

But I wasn't grand. I didn't get on the bike. It would get me home too fast. I pushed it along the road and I kept stopping and picking stuff out of the hedges and crushing leaves, and smelling what they smelled like.

Fourteen. All my curiosity about who my da was turned sour. I wasn't sure I wanted to know any more. It made me feel sick. If it was just some lad she knew at school she would have told me, I was sure of that. So it wasn't just some lad. It was someone else, some dirty old bastard who was bad enough to take advantage of a school kid.

I knew she wasn't the only one in the world. I heard of a girl in my school who had a kid when she was fourteen, and another two when they were fifteen. But that was the point. You heard about it because it was unusual and because it was terrible and it ruined their lives for them. My ma went back to school after I was born, and she did her Junior Cert and all, but after that she left and stayed at home with me in her ma's house. She had a job for a while until her ma said she was sick of minding me and my ma would have to take over again. When she was eighteen she got her own flat and that was it. That was her life so far. She never had time to enjoy herself. She never had a life of her own. Maybe it was no wonder she was useless.

When I went in she said: 'I'm not staying here after that. I can't stay in a house where a little girl was murdered.'

'I told you,' I said. 'You wouldn't listen.'

'You did not tell me!' she said.

'I told you it was haunted.'

'It is not haunted!' she shouted at me.

'Well, what are you worried about, then?' I said.

'We'll have to move,' she said. 'I can't stay here.'

I helped myself to a bar, then took another one. I was starving. 'It suits me,' I said. 'I never wanted to come down here in the first place.'

'I don't mean back to Dublin,' she said. 'I'm not going back there. We'll get another house. In Ennis, maybe. Near the shops. I'll get my deposit back off him.'

'Not all of it, you won't,' I said. 'You'll have to pay him for that mattress.'

I took the bars up to my room and ate them. Then I took the little spanner that Matty gave me out of my jacket. I put it on my locker, like I was the kind of fella who always found spanners in his pockets, and other things too, like spark plugs and sets of old points.

I lay down on my bed and took out my fags. When I counted them I realized I hadn't smoked a single one since I left the house to go up to the Dooleys'. I lit one now and started thinking about my ma again, but I didn't want to think about her so I thought about engines instead, and I dreamed about one then, a huge Volvo truck engine chugging away, and carrying me wherever I wanted to go.

I woke up really early, starving hungry. It wasn't light yet but it wasn't dark, either. The window was kind of grey. I thought of the drawing in Lars's book again and it scared the bejaysus out of me, but I knew I'd never get back to sleep unless I got something to eat.

The wind was noisy outside but everything in the house was quiet. The light was on in the kitchen and the little green bowl and a smeared glass were upside down on the draining board beside a heap of dirty dishes. The milk carton was empty and there was no more in the fridge. All the bars were gone.

'I'll fucking burst him,' I said.

I made my sandwich and I was about to go upstairs again but I seen Dennis through the window. He was out on the grass in his pyjamas, trying to make the dog chase a stick. I went out and got him.

'Come in, you little bollix,' I said to him, but I didn't kill him and I kept him quiet. If he woke my ma she'd go ballistic and I wanted to go back to sleep again. I sent Dennis back to his room and ate my sandwich in bed, but he was clattering around and making such a racket I was sure he was going to wake my ma. So I went and got him and made him come in with me. He kept whispering to himself and wriggling, and there was no way I could sleep. I shushed him and he went quiet for a bit. Then he said: 'Bobby?'

I said, 'What?'

'She says she used live here. She wants you and Mammy to go away.'

I went rigid in the bed. I couldn't even tell him to shut up.

'She has no husband and no babbies. There's no one left, only her, on her own. Isn't that very sad?'

I still couldn't answer. I couldn't even breathe. He said: 'I could marry her, couldn't I, Bobby? 'Cos I'm little, too.'

'No, Dennis,' I said, and suddenly I felt calm. It was going to be all right. 'You can't marry her 'cos we're going back to Dublin. You and me and Mammy. This place isn't right for us. We're all going home.'

He didn't say anything else and after a bit I realized he was gone asleep. But I stayed awake for ages, listening to the house, terrified of what I might hear downstairs.

When I woke up again a few hours later he was fast asleep in the middle of the bed and I was hanging out over the edge. I started thinking about what he said, but then I seen the little spanner on my locker and I remembered Matty and the brake blocks and all.

Any excuse to get out of that fucking house. I went out before my ma got up and I started thumbing it to Ennis. An old fella picked me up in an ancient VW Golf. He had a dog in there with him and he had to make it get off the front seat so I could get in. From the smell of the car, the dog lived in it.

But your man was decent enough. He didn't say much after we'd agreed about the weather, and he went out of his way to drop me off near the shopping centre. By then I'd already realized how stupid I was. It was only eleven o'clock and the shops wouldn't be open until two on a Sunday. I had three whole hours to kill.

I'd had my toast and I could make that last me through until I got home, but I hadn't had a cup of tea because there was no milk and I couldn't do without that. I was more addicted to tea than I was to fags. So I had to break my fiver to get a cup of tea, and once it was broke it was gone, so I had another one as well, and a scone, and then I went down by the river to stop myself from spending any more.

There were ducks floating around on the water. I threw a stone at one of them. I missed, and the duck went after it. It thought it was a bit of bread I was throwing for it, and it looked into the water and there was nothing there, and it made me break my arse laughing. I did it again and it worked a few more times, and all the ducks went paddling after my stones. But then they got wise to me and stopped chasing the stones, so I went back to trying to hit them again, and I got one on the neck and it quacked and flew away, and the others all went after it.

All that stuff with Dennis in the night kept trying to get into my head, but I wouldn't let it. I did what my ma did. I put my hands over my ears and made noises so I couldn't hear what I was thinking. I wandered down the river a bit and there were some swans with their heads under the water and their arses in the air. I threw a big rock in the middle of them and they soon came up again, but they didn't go away and it was better craic just watching them go under and come back up with their long necks like snakes and their mouths full of weeds.

When they went off I smoked a fag and chucked some big rocks in the water to see the splash. I still had two hours to wait. I was getting bored and I was afraid of what I might do if I went back into town, so I took out my phone and played the racing-car game for a while, and then I sent Beetle a text message.

back in dublin soon wot u up 2

Then I played the game again until the battery ran out. I never got an answer from Beetle.

46

I only had seven fags left by the time the shops opened. I went into the mall the back way so I didn't have to walk past the supermarket where I robbed the six-pack, but there was a security man beside the door and he watched me when I went in. Outside the car shop I stopped and looked back. He was still watching me.

'What you looking at?' I said. That was really stupid. I wished I hadn't said it.

I went into the shop and I was looking for the brake blocks, and then I wondered why I was bothering to get them at all. I never thought about it before, but if we were going back to Dublin I had no use for them. I was certain by then that we were going back. My ma would never get the money together for another month's rent in advance. She must have got the last lot off one of those money-lenders that were hassling her sister. Probably told them she wanted it for a holiday or something. She wouldn't know where to start looking for another one down here, and I couldn't see any other way she'd get that kind of money.

So I gave up on the brake blocks. But on my way out of the shop I seen something else, and as soon as I picked it up I knew I had to have it. I looked around the shop and it was quiet, but when I looked out the door that security fella was there, and he was still watching me.

I looked at the price and I didn't know whether to laugh or cry.

Twenty-nine, ninety-nine. Exactly what I had left. I went to the cash desk and handed over the last of my deposit money. I didn't want the one cent change, but I waited for it anyway. I wanted my receipt so I could shove it in the face of that gobshite outside. He wasn't watching me any more, but I showed it to him anyway.

'See?' I said. 'You stupid, culchie bastard.'

When I got home I showed my ma what I'd bought.

'It's a torque wrench,' I told her. 'You can set the torque on the handle here, look.'

'What do you want that for?' she asked me. 'You're not going robbing cars again, are you?'

'It's not for robbing cars,' I said. 'It's for fixing them.'

'What cars?' she said. 'We haven't even got a car.'

I didn't try to explain. I couldn't, really, not even to myself. I just wanted it.

I went up to my room and took it out of its box and put it on top of the chest of drawers and arranged all the socket heads around it. Then I called Dennis in to look at it. He was nervous coming into my room. He thought it was a trick, an ambush or something. I lifted him up and showed him.

'It's a torque wrench,' I said. 'Say "torque wrench".'

He said, 'Toc . . . Say it again?'

'Torque wrench.'

'Torque wrench,' he said.

'Good boy,' I said. 'Now don't you dare touch it. Not ever.'

He ran off, but I stood there another while, just looking at it. It was the best thing I'd owned in my whole life.

47

'So when are we leaving?' I said to my ma while we were having our tea.

'Oh, I don't know,' she said. 'I've changed my mind.'

'You've what?' I said.

'I've calmed down a bit now,' she said. 'And I've had a chance to think. This place is really cheap, you know, Bobby. Once my rent allowance comes through it'll cost us even less.'

'The flat in Dublin cost you next to nothing,' I said. 'It can't cost less than that.'

'Yeah, but look what we've got,' she said. 'Three bedrooms and that big sitting room and the wood fire. And you have your job up the road.'

'It's not a job,' I said. 'It's a punishment.'

'But you like it, though. I know you do. And you haven't been getting into trouble or anything. You're much happier here than you were in Dublin.'

'Where do you get that from?' I said. 'How many times do I have to tell you? I . . . want . . . to . . . live . . . in . . . Dublin. I . . . don't . . . want . . . to . . . live . . . here. OK?'

'It's better for you,' she said. 'It's better for all of us.'

I was ready to explode, but I knew that would get

me nowhere. 'Well, it's not so good for Dennis,' I said. 'He was outside when I came down this morning. Out in the grass in his bare feet.'

'It's good for him to be outside,' she said. 'Fresh air's good for him.'

'At five o'clock in the morning?' I said. 'And he finished all the milk. He gave it to his little woman. He thinks he's going to marry her.'

'No he doesn't,' she said. 'There is no little woman, is there, Dennis?'

'There is,' he said, but she wasn't about to listen to him.

'It's only a game. All kids have imaginary friends like that. I don't know why you want to make such a big deal about it.'

Then I did explode. 'You don't care!' I yelled at her. 'One child was murdered here already and you don't care if yours get murdered too!'

'Just shut up!' she yelled back. 'You're talking shite.'

Then suddenly I knew. I knew how to prove it to her, about the little woman.

'I'll show you,' I said. 'Just you wait there.'

She had moved Dennis's toothbrush from the door of the cupboard under the stairs and wedged it with a bit from a cereal box instead. I yanked it out and pulled open the door, and started pulling the stuff out again – the clothes and torn bin bags, the shoes. I threw them out behind me into the room.

'Stop it, Bobby!' she said. 'What are you doing?'

'I'm going show you,' I said. 'I'm going to prove it to you.'

I kept dragging, threw the two boxes out behind me, moved the computer out the way. Bits and pieces scattered all over the place.

'Get off that stuff!' she shouted. 'It's not ours. Leave it alone!'

I threw a box of books so hard it knocked Dennis over. My ma picked him up and went out, and slammed the door behind her. The diary was where I left it, wedged into the little hole in the wall. I dragged out the plastic bag and tipped the diary out.

It fell out with the pages open, and something small landed on the floor beside it. A bank card. I picked it up, and looked more closely at the diary. Inside the back cover was a flap, a little file thing that opened out when you pulled it. There were other things inside it. Two more bank cards. A driving licence. A passport. And five hundred and fifty euros in fifty-euro notes.

I was made up.

I put the valuables in my pocket. Then, quietly and carefully, I put all the other stuff back into the cupboard.

48

I was anxious hitching into town the next morning in case PJ or anyone else I knew passed by, but it was too early for any of them to be on the road and I got a lift from a young one in a suit who said she was a solicitor. By eight o'clock I was on the first bus out of Ennis, watching the fields go by. There were contractors in one of them, baling silage, but I would never have to do that again. I was sorted now. The five hundred and fifty was sure to be enough for a deposit on a room, and then there was the other stuff as well. The credit card would probably be good for an hour or two if I could find places where you still didn't need a PIN code. I wasn't sure about the driving licence, but I knew I'd heard Fluke talking about selling passports. Passports were brilliant things to get.

The smell of rashers in the café in Limerick was mouth-watering but I didn't let myself be tempted. I had a packet of biscuits from home and I made myself a big mug of tea before I left and I drank it going down the road and left it hanging on a branch when it was empty. There was no way I was going to break even one of those fifties before they were safely in a landlord's hands and I was set up for my new life in Dublin. This time I wasn't going to screw up.

I was on the Limerick bus and we were just leaving the city behind and speeding up on the main road when it hit me. What the passport meant, and the driving licence, and the cards and the money. It meant Lars had not set out like me to start a new life for himself where nobody could find him. He hadn't set out to go anywhere at all.

So what had happened to him?'

Just for a second, I was blinded by the shock of it. I was falling into a black hole and all I could think of to do was to try and put that thought back in its box, wherever it came from, and get back to the way I was before I ever had it. But it wouldn't go.

I told myself I didn't care what had happened to Lars. It was none of my business. I told myself a big fella like that would be well able to look after himself. I told myself there was no way it meant that two murders had happened in that house instead of one.

And for a minute I held on to my dream. My ma and Dennis would be OK. And anyway, I didn't care. I wouldn't even know what happened to them once I got myself set up in Dublin. And anyway, it was her decision. It wasn't my fault if there really was some psycho wandering around down there. She had been warned, after all. Plenty of times. I'd told her a million times.

But there were these other thoughts going round in my head, and I couldn't shut them out. Fourteen. She was only fourteen. I knew she wasn't, but she had been, when she had me. And there was Dennis, the little bollix. *She wants you and Mammy to go away. I could marry her, couldn't I, Bobby?*

And then I was up at the front of the bus and yelling at the driver to stop.

'No way I'm stopping now,' he said. 'You'll have to wait till we get to Limerick Junction.'

'You have to stop,' I said. 'Now! I'm going to puke all over your bus!'

He pulled over on to the hard shoulder and opened the door. I jumped out and ran back along the road like the guards were after me. No. I ran faster than if the guards were after me.

When I came in the door my ma flew at me and slapped me with both hands until I hit her back to stop her.

'What's wrong with you?' I said.

'Me?' she said. 'It's you, you dirty little bastard. Where have you been?'

'Ma, listen,' I said.

'No, you listen,' she said. 'Do you know where I found him this morning?'

'Dennis?' I said.

'I couldn't find him anywhere when I got up. It took me half an hour to find him. He was way over on that boggy field over there. He'd gone through three hedges. He was frightened out of his wits!'

'What was he doing there?' I said.

'I don't know. I don't care. He just keeps going on

and on about his little woman. And then as if that wasn't bad enough you go and piss off on me as well. I thought you were at work until Coley came looking for you.'

'Well I wasn't,' I said. 'I found Lars's passport.'

'You found what?' she said.

I showed her the passport and the cards and the driving licence, but I kept quiet about the five hundred and fifty euro. No one needed to know about that. She didn't seem to understand what it meant. She just looked at them.

'We have to tell someone about it,' I said. 'We have to get out of this house.'

I seen hope light up her face, and then fear, and I thought, *Fourteen.*

She said, 'I'm going to nail up the dog flap. That'll stop Dennis going out. I don't know why I didn't think of it before. The dog will just have to go back.'

I took the dog up to Dooley's on a string. It didn't want to go. When I got to the house I could see Coley over by his weanling sheds, laying out boards for a concrete apron. He waved at me but I didn't go over. I knocked on the door.

Margaret opened it. She didn't look one bit pleased to see me.

'You've decided to show up then, have you?' she said.

'I just brought the dog back,' I said. 'And I found these.'

I handed her the passport and stuff.

'What's this?' she said. Then she looked, and I could see her face changing when she realized what I'd given her.

'Where did you get these?' she said.

'I found them in the house,' I said. 'Inside an old diary.'

'My God,' she said. 'However the guards missed them. I'd better phone them again. You did the right thing to bring them up here.'

She went to close the door on me. I said: 'What'll I do with the dog?'

'Just leave him off,' she said. 'He'll be all right.'

I took the string off the dog. It followed me home. My ma was bringing in firewood.

'You were supposed to leave him there,' she said, laughing at me with the dog.

'He wouldn't stay,' I said.

'He loves us, don't you, Bimbo?' she said.

Bimbo wagged his tail and ran away from her, into the house. I told her Margaret was phoning the guards. She said: 'What for?'

'Because of the passport and stuff,' I said. 'It changes everything.'

'He probably just forgot to bring it with him,' she said. 'Wherever he went.'

'He's dead, Ma,' I told her.

'That's rubbish,' she said. 'You don't know that.'

'I do,' I said. 'I'm certain of it.'

I almost felt sorry for her. She was being made to choose between the money-lenders and something that could be even worse. But for the moment, at least, she was clinging on to her dream.

'Well I don't believe it,' she said. 'No way I'm going to go back to Dublin until I have to.'

But I was clinging to my dream, too. I found my ma's needle and thread in her room and I unpicked the lining of my jacket and stitched the fifty-euro notes inside it. All except one. One way or another I was getting out of there, and when the time came, I was going to need another bus ticket.

49

The guards arrived about two hours later. There were two of them at first, and they wanted to know where I'd found the passport and stuff. I told them about the hole in the wall under the stairs and I showed them the cupboard with all Lars's things in it, but they didn't touch it. They asked me what I was doing in there and for a minute I couldn't think, and then I remembered.

'Looking for the DVD cable,' I said. 'Mr Dooley said it might be in there.'

'Did you find anything else?' they asked me.

'Like what?' I said. 'There's loads of his stuff in there but I didn't touch it. I only moved it out of the way. I didn't steal anything, if that's what you mean.'

They said it wasn't, but I knew it was. Then some more guards arrived in a van, and we all had to go outside while they searched the house. I seen one of them carrying out the computer and then he went back in and came out with the diary and some other files and books and things, and he put them in the van, too. There were more guards searching the sheds and the hedges and walls around the house, and then another van arrived with more of them and about four dogs. They all set out in different directions, and after a while we were allowed go back inside. I was glad I hid the money in my jacket and not somewhere around the house. I'd say there was nothing they hadn't found, right down to Dennis's toenail clippings in the log basket.

My ma started packing as soon as she got in. She started with Dennis's clothes and toys and his DVDs that he never got to watch there. Dennis was diving under the duvet and trying to play Where's Dennis? with her, but she was ignoring him.

'He'll have to give me my deposit back,' she said. 'There's no way anyone's supposed to live in a place where someone's died or disappeared. He had no right letting it to us in the first place.'

I was delighted. I went and started packing my own things. My best clothes and my tools were already in my backpack from the morning. I stuffed whatever else I could get in there, then got a bin bag from my ma's roll and started putting things in that.

'Don't put your duvet in yet,' my ma said. 'We probably can't go until tomorrow, till we get the rent back and all.'

I could see her mind working. It wasn't just the deposit, now, it was the whole lot, everything she'd given PJ in the brown envelope, even though we'd been living there for more than two weeks and we'd ruined one of his mattresses. She was like that with money. She always thought it would be there in the future, even though it never was. If Carmel saw twenty of it she'd be doing well. And there was no way in the world it would go back where it came from, to the money-lenders. I could see my ma spending it already, in her mind's eye.

There was a knock at the door and I ran down to get it. It was Coley.

'They found him,' he said, but he didn't sound excited or anything. He just looked serious.

'Who is it?' my ma said from upstairs.

'It's Coley,' I said. 'They found him, Ma.'

Coley led us over the stile and we walked up across the rushy fields with him. On the way he said to me: 'Fair play to you for finding the passport and handing it over and all. That was the right thing to do.'

'What else did you think I would do?' I said.

He laughed. 'You'd never know with you.'

When we were halfway up the second field Coley stopped and turned round.

'We could see from the house,' he said.

He pointed down the hill, across the road from our house and in a bit, to the muddy field where Kevin Talty kept his cattle in the winter. The guards had taped off an area around the feeder and they were all standing outside it, doing nothing.

'They'll be waiting for forensics,' said Coley. 'Or maybe the state pathologist or something.'

'Maybe they found something else?' my ma said. 'His jacket or something?'

'Maybe,' said Coley. 'But if they did there's an awful lot of fellas standing around looking at it.'

We stayed and watched for a while but it had

started raining, and anyway there was nothing to see, so my ma said we'd be better off at home.

'Tell your da we're leaving in the morning,' she said to Coley. 'And ask him can we have our deposit back, and the rent we paid in advance.'

Coley was already walking up the field towards his house. He didn't even look back.

'I'll tell him,' he said.

When my ma got in she phoned Carmel and told her what was happening. They were happy as Larry when they were talking about the murder, but when my ma said we were coming back and had nowhere to stay it turned into a screaming match again.

'Well, where else can we go?' my ma said, and, 'I'll have the fucking money. He's giving it me back. Yeah. All of it, so you can stop shitting yourself.' And, 'It's only a couple of days, for God's sake! Just while we get ourselves sorted.' And, 'I never thought my own sister would turn me away. Our ma will be turning in her grave.'

After that she hung up and said to me, all smiles again, 'That's sorted, then. We're staying with Carmel.'

She sent a couple of text messages, then went back to her packing, but a few minutes later PJ arrived at the door. I could tell the minute I seen him that he was raging. There was steam rising up off his bald patch.

'Coley tells me you're leaving,' he said to my ma.

'That's right,' she said. 'First thing in the morning if we can find a way in to the bus.'

'Oh, I'll bring you in,' PJ said. 'You need have no worries on that account. But there's no way I'm giving you any money back.'

My ma stared at him. 'What do you mean?' she said. 'I gave you a deposit and all, and a month in advance. We haven't been here anywhere near a month.'

'And your son stole a car the day after you arrived,' he said. 'Have you forgotten that? The whole of what you gave me is nowhere near paying it back. I was willing to give you the benefit of the doubt and let him work it off, but since you're walking out I can't get it that way, can I? I'm going to have to find it somewhere and give it to that poor lad's mother.' He pointed out the window in the direction of where they had found Lars.

'Oh,' my ma said. 'We'll pay that off separately, won't we, Bobby? I'll send it down to you every week until . . .'

But PJ was shaking his head. 'You can do that for what you still owe me, but I'm keeping what I have.'

'But we need it,' my ma said. 'We have to get another flat and I need the deposit for that. I'll be back on the bottom of the waiting list. We have nowhere to go.'

He moved towards the door. My ma went after him. 'You have to give it back. We haven't even got enough for our bus fare. I haven't a penny until Thursday.'

He turned back and took out his wallet, and threw fifty euro on the table.

'I'll be here in the morning to pick you up,' he said. 'I'll be here at half eight. Don't keep me waiting.'

My ma said, 'Oh please, Mr Dooley. I really need that money! We'll send you the money for the car, honest!' She started turning on the waterworks but PJ just looked at her.

'The guards have just found a body,' he said. 'Lars was a nice fella. He was dead sound.'

Then he left, and my ma took it all out on me.

50

She was on the rampage all evening. After the first bit when she went through me for a shortcut I stayed out of her way, but Dennis had a terrible time of it. He went up to bed early in the end. He volunteered to go.

When it got dark my ma bolted the front door and piled up chairs against the back one. She said she wasn't going to sleep that night but she dozed off in front of the TV before midnight, and when she did I crept out into the kitchen. I took all the chairs away, put out some milk and biscuits on the window ledge, then piled all the chairs back up again.

I'd only just finished doing it when my phone rang. I nearly jumped out of my skin.

It was Coley.

'He was dismembered,' he said. 'Hacked into little pieces with a blunt knife.'

The hairs stood up on the back of my neck. 'How do you know?' I said.

'Tom has friends in the guards. They said whoever killed him buried him in the mud around the cattle feeder, and the cattle were treading him in deeper all spring.'

'Oh, God,' I said.

'Yeah,' he said. 'Creepy, isn't it?'

'Do they know who did it?' I said.

'They've taken Kevin Talty in for questioning but there's no way in the world he did it. He's a bit eccentric all right, but he wouldn't hurt a fly. And they're getting in a translator to look at Lars's emails and his diary, because everything's in Swedish. There might be something in one of those.'

'Lars seen a little woman,' I said. 'And my brother seen her, too.'

'A little woman?' he said. 'How do you know Lars saw her?'

'It was in his diary,' I said.

'Can you read Swedish?'

'No,' I said. It was too complicated to explain.

He laughed, and I nearly hung up, but then he said: 'Anyway, it's a shame you're leaving.'

'Why?' I said.

'My father was going to buy you an old banger to fix up, and Matty said he'd help you. My father said it would be something to give you an interest, like.'

'I've loads of interests,' I said, but something in me was hurting – that pain under my ribs – and it pushed its way up into my throat like a fist and I couldn't push it back down again.

'I might be up in Dublin some time,' he said. 'I might look you up.'

'Do that,' I said, and I hung up.

I didn't sleep much in the night and nor did my ma. I

heard her moving around in the kitchen and standing in the front porch, listening. But she wasn't awake when Dennis came creeping out of his room and along the landing. I caught him going down the stairs, but he wasn't going looking for his little woman. His arms were full of soaking bedclothes and he was so scared his breath was squeaking.

'Shh,' I said. 'Show me them.'

He gave them to me and we took them down to the bathroom and rinsed them out, duvet and all, and hung them over the shower rail to drip. Then I found a clean pair of shorts and a T-shirt for him in the top of one of the bags, and I helped him change into them, and brought him back up into my room to sleep with me.

'Bobby?' he whispered when we settled in.

'What?'

'I like the torque wrench,' he said. 'It's brilliant, isn't it?'

He got it in the neck from my ma anyway, even though she didn't need to clean up after him.

We were all up early, to be ready when PJ came to pick us up. The kitchen was in the usual mess and I said to my ma, 'Aren't you going to wash up? You can't leave the place like this.'

'Why not?' she said. 'Why should I do anything for that thieving bastard? He can't do that, you know. He can't refuse to give me my deposit back. I'll have the law on him.'

But it wasn't for PJ that I washed up the dishes myself, and dried them and put them all away. I just couldn't stand to picture the looks on their faces, him and Margaret. I couldn't stand to think of what they would say about my ma.

51

I thought at least I'd have Fluke's room, even if I had to share it with Dennis. But Fluke was back and living with his ma again already.

'I must have been off my head,' he said. 'Moving in with a woman with two kids. It was fucking pandemonium. And she was only after my wallet, like all of them. She expected me to get shopping and stuff, out of my own dole. I told her where to stick it.'

Carmel was gobsmacked when she heard my ma didn't get the money. She said she should bring a case in the small claims court but then my ma had to tell her about paying him back for the car, and then Carmel went ballistic. My ma started crying, and then Carmel said she'd bring her down to Debtbusters in the morning and see if they could sort out something to get the money-lenders off her back, and my ma cheered up a bit then. I couldn't see it working, though. She had been down there twice before and she never paid off the loans she got from them those times. There was only so much they could do.

I couldn't stand being in the flat with everybody arguing all the time, so I went out to start looking for my own place. Now the idea was in my head I couldn't let it go. Even if my ma did find a new flat there was no way

I was going living with her any more. I bought a newspaper and went through all the ads in the back of it and
I rang loads of people, but nobody would even show me
a room, let alone rent me one. They said the place was
already gone, or they were looking for a 'mature
professional', whatever that is, or they only wanted girls.
And they all wanted stupid money as well. I thought I
was made up with five-fifty, but they wanted that much
for a month, and the same again as a deposit. I wasn't
about to give up, though. I knew I could swing it somehow. If I found the place I could find the money. I kept
ringing numbers. My phone ran out of credit and I had
to break my fifty euro to get more. But that was OK. I
had to live while I was looking.

When the evening paper came out there were some
new ads in it, and this time when I phoned them I said I
was a student. One fella said he'd show me a room at
four o'clock and I went all the way out to Dollymount
on the bus to see it. There were fifteen other people there
before me, all of them waiting to see the same room, and
he gave it to a slapper who smiled at him the right way.
They're total bastards, those landlords. They have no
respect for people.

I was on the bus going back in when Coley rang me
again. He said the guards had sent dogs down the badger
hole in the fort and a badger ran out the other end where
it comes out the side of the hill. He said the guards
all stood around looking in the hole and one of them
took his jacket off and rolled up his sleeves and went

down on his knees and shone a torch into the hole like he was going to go down into it. But then he got up and put his jacket on again, and now they were digging their way in through the top of it. He was laughing like it was the funniest thing he ever seen, but I wouldn't have gone headfirst down that hole if you gave me a Mercedes.

I was glad he rang me. I thought he didn't like me, after all the things that had happened, but he must have, or he wouldn't have phoned. I thought of him standing up there beside his sheds and watching all that was going on. He had a grandstand view up there on the hill. Holy Coley. He wasn't the worst, I suppose. I thought of the hay and the silage and the bullocks and the drains we dug together. But things could happen in Dublin as well, and I was going to make sure they did.

When I got back to the flats I hung around outside until a few lads my own age came along, and I got talking to them. We swapped scars and stories first, the usual pissing contest, and then I asked them if they wanted to go out and try and find a bit of action. They all said they did and they looked dead keen, but when I turned up to meet them at half eleven there was only one of them there, and he was a few hoops short of a barrel. I wasn't going anywhere on my own with him.

In the morning the guards arrived at the door to finger-print Dennis. That's the truth. I nearly fell off the floor when I heard that. But when I heard why it was nearly worse. They had gone into the badger hole and there were two big stone rooms down there under the ground, and they found a knife there with old blood stains and some small little fingerprints. The only child within miles with hands that size was Dennis.

'Well he never done it,' Carmel said. My ma wasn't there at the time. She was down at Debtbusters.

'We know that,' they said. 'It's just for the purposes of elimination, that's all.'

They said they found chocolate wrappers in there. 'He might have found his way in there some time. Did you, Dennis? Eh? Did you go into a hole in the ground? A little cave?'

Dennis shook his head. They took his fingerprints and he cried while they were doing it but afterwards he liked it that his fingers were all black and he kept saying, 'Look, look,' to everybody, even the guards.

After they done the fingerprints they showed us a torch, and a blue shirt inside a plastic evidence bag and they asked if either of us seen them before. I said no, but Dennis pointed at the shirt and said: 'It's a dress,' and then I seen it was the one Lars had been wearing in Margaret Dooley's photograph album.

'What do you mean, it's a dress?' the guard said to Dennis. But Dennis wasn't saying anything else.

Then they asked me if I seen anything strange around there. A small person, perhaps. I said I hadn't. So they asked Dennis.

'Did you see a little woman, Dennis? Maybe you thought it was another child, like yourself?'

But Dennis said nothing, no matter how sweetly they asked him. He was only four years old but already he knew how to deal with the guards.

52

I woke up in the morning with a memory of something I seen. I thought I seen it anyway, or maybe it was just a dream, but it was a sign in a window of a house saying ROOM TO RENT. NO STUDENTS. Or something like that. I thought maybe I seen loads of signs like that, and maybe that was the way to get cheap rooms, from people who didn't have the money to advertise in the paper. So I went out as soon as I got up and just started walking, and looking in all the windows.

I missed my bike. Walking was too slow, and too boring. But after a while my mind started buzzing and I had to keep reminding myself to look out for the signs, because there was so much going round in my head about the little woman and the blue dress and a child who bawled like a kid goat and a man cut into little pieces by a knife with tiny fingerprints on it.

It was what the guards said made me realize it. *A small person.* And what they said to Dennis. *Maybe you thought it was another child.* Then I couldn't believe I never thought of it before.

I rang Coley. It was the first time I ever rang him.

'Coley,' I said. 'I figured it out.'

'Figured what out?' he said.

'Who killed Lars. It was Peggy's daughter.'

He went quiet.

'She was never murdered at all? She went back to live in the fort, and then when Joe came back he looked after her, and then he made your grandma leave out milk for her after he died.'

Coley was laughing.

'No,' I said. 'It's right. She turned into the little woman that Lars seen. And Dennis seen her as well.'

'What are you on?' Coley said. 'Are you smoking wacky baccy up there?'

'No, Coley,' I said. 'She really was swapped when she was a babby, see. By the fairies. Ask your grandma. She'll tell you.'

'Don't mind my grandmother,' Coley said. 'Whoever killed Lars, I don't think it was a fairy.'

I hung up on him. I was raging. I wanted to prove I was right, and I nearly phoned the guards myself, to tell them. That'd teach Coley. That would stop him fucking laughing. But I nearly laughed at myself, then, at the idea of me phoning the guards.

I never seen a single sign in a window, not one. So I got the newspaper again and rang some more numbers, but it was the same old story. I was just wasting my credit. If I went on like this I would have to start into the five hundred I'd stitched into my jacket. No way I was doing that.

So I thought I'd try word of mouth instead and I rang Beetle. He said he didn't know any rooms going but the way to find one was to look on the Internet. There was a great website that had new places listed every few minutes, he said.

'Come round to my place tomorrow and you can use my computer.'

'I can come now,' I said. 'I can be there in half an hour.'

'I'm not at home,' he said. 'Come at two o'clock tomorrow. I'll be there.'

I was going to ask him where he was and if we could hook up, but he rang off and the phone was just dead in my hand.

A few minutes later I found out why. I was waiting for my bus and I seen him over the other side of the road with Fluke and some little kid I never seen before. I went across the road.

'Where you heading?' I said to them.

'Just chilling,' Fluke said. 'Just going in to have a look around.'

I looked at the little kid. He was only about eleven, skinnier even than me, but he looked hard. And I suddenly knew what he was doing there with them. He was their new bag-snatcher and carrier. He was taking over from me.

So where did that leave me? If Fluke sold the goods and Beetle bought the gear, did that mean I was their new psycho Mick? No way. But I said: 'Suits me. Where shall we go?'

'We're not going with you,' Fluke said. 'Not after what you done to Mick.'

'I didn't do nothing to Mick,' I said. 'All I done was get the car.'

'It's all the same,' Fluke said. 'The guards have your number. If they catch us with you we'll all go down.'

'Who's going to catch us?' I said, but Fluke wasn't listening.

'Fuck off, Bobby,' he said. 'Go find your own trouble.'

'See you tomorrow,' Beetle said. 'Two o'clock.'

He looked embarrassed but that only made me feel worse. I stood on the street and watched them walk away. The little kid muscled in between them like he had every right to be there, even though he had to take two steps for every one they did.

I couldn't believe it. I couldn't believe this was happening. I ran up the street pushing bins over, kicking cars, setting off alarms, smashing wing mirrors. Then I ran down the back lanes until I was lost to myself, as well as to the guards.

I wanted to get off my head. Anything would do it – the stronger the better. I knew where I could buy gear – not serious gear like Beetle could get, but good enough to take the pain away for a while. But on my way back to the next bus stop I felt the fifty-euro notes, all scrunched up in the lining of my jacket. There was no way I was breaking into them, no matter how bad I felt.

In my jeans pocket I had twenty-seven euro. I got off the bus two stops before the flats and went to a

corner shop I knew where the fella would sell you anything you wanted as long as you had the money, ID or
no ID. I got twenty smokes and two bottles of cider, and
they kept me out of it until bedtime.

Fluke came in hammered and fell over me. I lashed out
at his head but it was a mistake. He was four years older
than me and twice as heavy, and he left me with a split
lip and a black eye.

It was never dark in Dublin, not like it was in Clare,
where the windows at night were like wet blackboards.
Here there was always light, that weird orange glow
from the street lamps. I could see well enough to reach
for a dirty T-shirt and wipe the blood off my mouth.

'I don't even fucking want you here,' Fluke said.
'You or your ma. You're a total waste of space, the lot
of you. You should be put to sleep. Put us all out of your
misery.'

He thought he was funny. He laughed at himself.

I was lying on three fat cushions from Carmel's
kitchen chairs. It was like trying to sleep on a row of
speed bumps. I pulled my duvet up over my head but I
could still hear Fluke ranting on.

'You should have stayed down in Clare and let the
psycho get you. We'd all be better off then.'

'I wish we had fucking stayed,' I said. 'The stink in
this room would nearly gas you.'

He rolled out of bed and kicked me on the hip. He
was still bigger and heavier than me, but he wasn't on

top of me now. I got up, quickly. He was drunk and off balance, and he was just sitting back down on his bed when I grabbed his CD player and smashed it into his face as hard as I could. He screamed and grabbed at his nose, and blood ran between his fingers, all black in the orange light.

I picked up my jacket and trainers and ran, straight out the flat and down the stairs into the night.

53

I wanted to rob a car. I wanted the buzz of driving too fast, the pure adrenaline rush that was the best way in the world of forgetting your problems. But I didn't have the energy to go looking for keys on my own. Beetle could smell an open door or an unwatched jacket a mile away, but I never could. So I stayed out for the rest of the night, walking the streets around my own part of town, backwards and forwards.

A fella asked me if I wanted tablets. Two hours later I passed him again and he asked me the same thing. I did want tablets, but I wanted a place of my own, away from Fluke, away from his ma and my ma screaming at each other all through the day and night. My five hundred was staying where it was and there was no way I was going to touch it, even if I had to starve.

I wasn't scared of Dublin at night. I belonged there. But she didn't, the little woman. I kept seeing here everywhere, out the corner of my eye, like she was following me. I knew she wasn't really there, but all the same it scared the shite out of me.

I wondered how she killed Lars, when he was so big and she was so small. He had a torch which the guards found. He must have gone in the hole after her, wearing his blue shirt. It wouldn't have been hard for her to kill him once he had his head down that hole. All she needed to do was to stick him in the right place in his throat and wait for him to bleed to death. After that she had to cut him into small pieces so she could carry them across the road and bury them under the mud around the cattle feeder. It must have been some night's work for a person the size of Dennis.

I was glad Coley didn't believe me. I didn't want the guards finding her, even if they could. I thought of what her life must have been like, living under the ground like that. She was all on her own, Dennis said so. All on her own, with nothing but darkness, day and night.

I couldn't get it out of my head, what I done to Fluke. My own cousin. I kept saying to myself that I never meant to do it, that I never meant to hit him so hard, but it wasn't true. When I hit him I wanted to hurt him. Maybe I even wanted to kill him, for what he done to me, pushing me out of the gang and that, treating me like a kid and bringing in that other lad and never saying a word about it. And when I thought about the way I went mental I couldn't help thinking about Psycho Mick, and how maybe that was what I'd turned into, because of what I said about him to the guards.

I seen the little woman again, looking into a rubbish bin, but it was just a dog, and it ran off when it seen me. I wondered where she was now. Out in the dark without a home, the same as myself. I felt sorry for her. She didn't set out to kill Lars any more than I set out to smash Fluke's face. If he'd left her alone and not gone after her she wouldn't have hurt him. She wouldn't have hurt Dennis, neither. He wasn't after her like Lars was. He was her little friend and he got her milk for her and gave her biscuits and small little squares of pink and yellow cake.

And I gave her Roses. No wonder she wanted more of them. Imagine what chocolate must taste like to someone who spends all their life eating beetles and worms.

I didn't even notice the morning coming until I passed a café that was open. I still had about eight euro left, and I got a full Irish breakfast for that, including toast and a whole pot of tea.

'What happened to the other fella?' the man behind the counter asked me.

'What?' I said.

He sent me into the jacks to look in the mirror. I had a massive shiner and my lip was swollen out like Mick Jagger. I thought it looked cool, but I wished it hadn't happened now. It wouldn't help my chances of getting a room.

'I fell off my bike,' I told him when he asked me again. I didn't want to think about what happened to the other fella. I remembered the blood coming through Fluke's fingers.

After my breakfast I wandered around a bit more, but I didn't want to go too far because I had to go to Beetle's in the afternoon. So when the sun had warmed up the air a bit I went into the park and went asleep under a bush. I kept my jacket on instead of using it as a blanket like I usually did. I didn't want some scumbag robbing it with all that money in the lining.

My ma rang me about half ten.

'Where are you, you little bollix?' she said.

'I'm asleep,' I said.

'Where?' she said. 'Carmel's been in the hospital all night with Luke. He's got a broken nose and eleven stitches in his face. What did you do to him?'

'He started it,' I said.

'Oh, Bobby,' she said. 'What am I going to do with you?'

'Nothing,' I said. 'Just leave me alone.'

I couldn't sleep again after that. I walked around the streets until my smokes were all gone and then I went round to Beetle's. I was early, and his da had to get him up out of bed.

'You can go back to sleep if you want to,' I told him. 'Just show me that website first.'

54

Three days later I landed up at the flat. My ma opened the door.

'Where the hell have you been?' she said.

I wanted to answer her but my mouth was busy, grinding my teeth or something. And anyway, I didn't know.

I lay down on the sofa and I thought I was awake all day, watching the white walls bending and stretching, but my ma told me later that she tried to wake me twice and I didn't know who she was.

But I knew who she was when I got up, and I knew as well that my whole five hundred euro was gone up in smoke.

Me and Beetle must have had a brilliant time.

'He can't stay here,' Carmel told my ma when she came in. 'Not after what he done to Luke. Look at the state of him!'

'Well what can I do?' my ma said. 'He won't take any notice of anything I say.'

'He should be locked up,' Carmel said. 'He should be in a mental home.'

'Don't be ridiculous,' my ma said. 'He's not that bad.'

'Well I don't care,' Carmel said. 'I couldn't give a shite what happens to him at this stage. All I know is he's not staying here.'

'Well what's he going to do then?' my ma said. 'Where's he supposed to go?'

I was lying on the couch again, and that question wouldn't leave me alone. It kept ringing through my head all night, whether I was awake or asleep.

'Where's he supposed to go?'

I heard Fluke come in and storm around the house, slamming doors and swearing. I heard Carmel yelling at him to leave me alone.

'Where's he supposed to go?'

I heard my ma laughing with her sister, and then rowing with her, and then I heard her screaming at Dennis, and I went back to sleep. Someone came in and turned on the TV. Someone else came in and turned it off again.

'Where's he supposed to go?'

I heard Dennis crying outside the bathroom door. I heard sirens speeding through the night and lads down in the courtyard, saying goodnight to each other in broad daylight.

'Where's he supposed to go?'

I was awake now, and I knew the answer.

I got up off the sofa and put my shoes on and felt down the back of it and got a two euro and a twenty-cent piece. There was another euro down the back of the armchair, but I still had a long way to go.

I got seven in change out of Carmel's purse that she left in the kitchen – some people never learn – and another one-fifty in small change out the bottom of a jar which had pens and rulers in it. Still not enough. It would have to do.

Fluke's door was open. He was snoring through his broken nose. I didn't look at his face. I pulled my back-pack out from under the pile of clothes and cushions on the floor. It still had everything I needed in it – my tools, my toothbrush, my clean clothes. I hadn't opened it since we arrived. I must have smelled like a drain, but I wasn't going to change now. I could do it somewhere along the way. I knew I was pushing my luck but I reached for Fluke's jeans. Coins clinked in the pocket but he didn't wake up. I put my hand in the pocket. There was a note in there as well as the coins. I closed my fist around the lot and backed out of the room with my bag.

And I was gone.

55

The garda tape was still up around the ring fort, and the hole in the middle of it gaped open, all black and silent. No way the little woman would be going back there any more. Would she find another place, another safe hole in the ground, where she could be a little woman again? Or would she stay a badger for ever, a creature of the night?

Was it the same with me? I was homeless, driven out because of what I done. Maybe that would be my future as well, being a creature of the night, mixing with others like me. But maybe, just maybe, I had one last chance.

Margaret opened the door to me. She got a shock when she seen me and she didn't even say hello. She just called back over her shoulder for PJ.

He looked older. They both did. And there was something else different about them as well, like they had lost some of their trust in people. Maybe it was me that robbed it off them. Maybe I needed it for myself.

'Hello, Bobby,' PJ said. 'What are you doing here?'

'I had to come, didn't I?' I said. 'I haven't finished paying off the car.'

They both looked at me and I knew what they were seeing. The black eye, the split lip, the way my skin would be looking after those three days on the gear. I seen Coley behind them, just his head poking out round the kitchen door.

That pain was inside my ribs again and I kept swallowing and swallowing but it wouldn't go back down. I looked back at PJ. He pulled in a long, deep breath and it took him ages, as if all the clean air of Clare wasn't enough to fill him. And when he let it out again he said: 'All right, Bobby. I suppose we'd better let you in.'

EPILOGUE

One time I had a tooth pulled out and for ages afterwards there was a hole in my gum and I couldn't keep my tongue out of it. I just kept poking away at it all the time. The Dooleys planted trees around the ring fort but the hole in the ground is still there, and my mind keeps poking away at it like the hole where the tooth was. I can't leave it alone. The little woman has a track worn for herself in my brain.

I been in a lot of places where I couldn't sleep. Wings, wards, dormitories. Troubled people make a lot of noise at night. There were times when I made a lot of noise myself, trying to beat a way through. Trying to fight myself instead of everyone else.

Sometimes in the darkness I seen loads of little people marching across Ireland and dancing in the fairy forts, but I know those times were dreams or flashbacks. But then I think maybe there were loads of them out there, even if I didn't see them. Maybe Ireland is teeming with little people, half badger, living under the ground. Or maybe Dennis's little woman was the last of them. What if her parents swapped her for Peggy's babby and went and died themselves, and she was the very last of her kind in the whole of Ireland?

I heard Dennis talking downstairs in Joe and

Peggy's old house, and I know that wasn't any dream. I heard the dog flap rattle. I seen a badger running away through the hedge. A badger. Maybe that's all it was. But I feel her terror, being driven away from the only place where she felt safe, and I feel Lars's terror when he sees her with that little knife in her hand coming towards him, and he realizes he's stuck with his head down the hole and he can't get out.

How long would it take to bleed to death?

Then I remember that it's all mad stuff and I don't believe any of it. And then I start back at the beginning again, and my head goes round and round, same old paths, same old thoughts.

Dennis was fourteen last week, and the number rang all kinds of bells for me. It seemed important for me to see him, so I picked him up and drove him down to Clare.

'To visit that place where we stayed,' I told him. 'To see how much you remember.'

We went to Dooleys' first but there was no one in. I was half disappointed and half relieved. The last time I was there was for Grandma Dooley's funeral a couple of years back, and PJ had a few too many and said a lot of embarrassing things about me to anyone who would listen. He thinks the world of me, PJ does, no matter how many times I let him down.

We drove on up to the top of the hill and looked down at Joe and Peggy's house from there. The forestry is over my head now, but they didn't plant inside the ring fort and you can still see it, just about. The hole is kind of healed around the edges by grass and stuff, but still black and gaping. It still gives me the creeps.

'Remember?' I said to Dennis.

He just shrugged. He isn't like me, Dennis. He's kind of slow and dreamy, not wild at all. He goes to school every day but I don't think he's up to much there. He has some kind of special classes, I think, but he doesn't talk about it. Not to me, anyway.

We drove down to the house. The Dooleys sold it to some young German people and they turned the stone shed into a workshop or studio or something, with lots of glass. There were apple trees and vegetable gardens and a polytunnel, but the house was pretty much the same as when we had it. From the outside, anyway.

'Remember it now?' I said.

He shook his head. There didn't seem to be anyone home so we went in around the back. There was no green bowl outside the window. There was a new back door with no dog flap. I tried the handle but it was locked. Not that it would be so hard to break in. I stepped back and looked up at the window in the gable end.

'That was my room,' I said to Dennis. 'You had a small little room under the roof.'

He looked across at the orchard. Some of the trees still had bits of white blossom. Beyond them the edge of the forestry was like a black wall. I didn't know if it was the right thing to do, put trees there. I went to go over and have a look, but I got a sudden notion that I might see a path, a little animal track disappearing in among the trees, and I changed my mind.

'You don't remember the dog?' I said. 'The little woman? The guy who was murdered?'

'I remember getting my fingerprints taken.' He held up his fingers and looked at the tips of them. 'I remember the black ink.'

They never got anyone for Lars's murder. They interviewed Kevin Talty three times but they never charged him. Doesn't mean he didn't do it.

But the fingerprints on the bloody knife. Tiny fingerprints. They didn't match Dennis's.

'I remember something else,' he said. 'I think I do.'

'What?' I almost didn't want to hear.

'A spanner,' he said. 'No, not a spanner. A torque wrench. Is that mad?'

I laughed at him. 'No. Not mad. There was a torque wrench.'

I still have it, that torque wrench, but I don't keep it in with my other tools. It was cheap and useless. It broke the third time I used it. But I keep it anyway, to remind me that it was once the most important thing in the world to me. And in a way, it still is.

'Show me your fingers again,' I said to Dennis. He held them up, pink and soft and clean.

I showed him mine, and he looked close, at the black grease deeply ingrained in all the little lines. It made me laugh. If I had a nice ham sandwich now, I could probably leave a decent pawprint in it.

THE NEW POLICEMAN
Kate Thompson

There is never enough time in Kinvara. When Helen Liddy is asked what she wants for her birthday, she says, 'Time. That's what I want. Time.'

Fifteen year-old JJ is continuing the Liddy family tradition with his fiddle-playing. But one day he discovers that music might not be the only thing that runs in his veins. Can it be true that his great-grandfather was a murderer?

When JJ sets out to buy his mother some time he discovers the answer, as well as some truly remarkable things about music, myth and magic.

Who knows where the time goes?

JJ does.

Winner of the Whitbread Children's Book Award and the 2005 Guardian Children's Fiction Prize

978 0 099 45627 8

THE LAST OF THE HIGH KINGS
Kate Thompson

JJ Liddy sometimes blames his unreliable temperament
on the visit he made to Tír na n'Óg, the land of eternal
youth, when he was fifteen years old. It's perhaps not
surprising that his children have also turned out to be
a little eccentric, especially eleven-year-old Jenny.
She forgets to go to school, can't bear to wear shoes,
and spends entire days roaming the mountainside.

It's up there that she meets the ghost. He is guarding
a pile of rocks known as the beacon, and when some
archaeologists arrive to evacuate it, they run into the
strangest kind of obstruction.

But it is not people the ghost fears, and when the
real enemy finally reveals itself, the future of the
entire human race is threatened. Only Aengus Óg
and his fairy kin can help now.

But why should fairies bother themselves
with human affairs?

978 1 862 30303 4

THE FOURTH HORSEMAN
Kate Thompson

The white rider had returned.
And this time he wasn't alone.

Should you believe what you see with your own eyes,
even if it can't be explained?

When Laurie is arrested for setting fire to her
father's research lab she's unsure what to say in
her defence. Should she say that she's an animal
rights activist? Or should she tell the whole story,
about the mysterious horseman that she saw in
the woods, and the terrifying truth which lay behind
their appearance? In the eyes of the police she
is a criminal. But Laurie knows that she's a hero.

A haunting story about modern science, religious
fundamentalism and the human thirst for power
from multi award-winning author Kate Thompson.

978 0 099 49503 1

THE BEGUILERS
Kate Thompson

Every night they come drifting through the
sky above the village streets, issuing their
mournful cries and terrorising the population.
It isn't safe to go out after dark

Everyone is aware of the power of the beguilers
but no one knows what they are. No one has ever
caught one. But every generation produces a
beguiler-hunter: a tragic soul considered by
the rest of the villagers to be insane.

Rilka isn't mad. But the desire to catch a beguiler
is about to change her life and the lives of those
around her, for ever.

WINNER OF THE BISTO BOOK OF THE YEAR AWARD

978 0 099 41149 9

THE SWITCHERS TRILOGY
Kate Thompson

Tess is a Switcher – someone who can change shape
to become another creature at the bat of an eyelid.
Then she discovers she shares this gift with Kevin
and that together they have powers beyond belief,
enabling the two of them to save the world from icy
destruction. But there are other more sinister characters
among the Switchers, and when Tess is dragged into
the dark night-time world of Martin, she finds herself
facing the most terrifying choice of her life.

A tremendous, unputdownable read.
Here in one dramatic volume are the three
Bestselling Switcher novels.

'Unmissable . . . spellbinding' *Sunday Telegraph*

978 0 099 47283 4